POISON

Also available from

SARAH PINBOROUGH & TITAN BOOKS

Charm

Beauty

POISON

A WICKED *SNOW WHITE* TALE

SARAH PINBOROUGH

TITAN BOOKS

Poison
Print edition ISBN: 9781783291076
E-book edition ISBN: 9781783291106

Published by Titan Books
A division of Titan Publishing Group Ltd
144 Southwark Street, London SE1 0UP

First edition: March 2015
2 4 6 8 10 9 7 5 3 1

Copyright © Sarah Pinborough 2013, 2015. All rights reserved.
First published by The Orion Publishing Group, London, 2013

A CIP catalogue record for this title is available from the British Library.

Printed and bound in Spain.

FOR PAUL KANE & MARIE O'REGAN,
Seeing how happy you two are gives me faith in true love
(that can, to be fair, be a mean feat at times!)

POISON

1

'Air and earth. Light and dark'

'She's too old for that nickname,' the queen said. She was standing at the window of the royal bedchamber and looking down at the courtyard below. Morning sun beat on the ground, but the air was still chilly. She shivered. 'She needs to start behaving like a lady. A princess.'

'She's young. There's time enough for that yet. And anyway,' the king laughed – a throaty sound that could have been born in the bowels of the earth or in the mud of the battlefield. 'You gave it to her.' He hauled himself out of bed and his footsteps were heavy. *He* was heavy. Getting heavier too. She'd married a glutton.

'She's not that young. Only four years younger than me,' the queen muttered. From behind her came the sound of liquid hitting ceramic and for the thousandth time she wished he'd have the good grace to at least piss in a different room. 'It was simply a passing remark that she was pale. It wasn't a compliment. It was meant to be a joke.' Her quiet words went unheard as her husband continued noisily with his bodily functions. 'And it was a long time ago,' she whispered, bitterly.

She watched as, far below, the young woman dismounted from her horse. She wore brown breeches and rode with her long legs astride the beast like a man. Her shirt was loose but, as the light breeze touched it, it clung to her slim form, flowing over the curve of her full breasts onto her flat stomach. Her thick raven hair fell around her shoulders and as she handed the reins of her stallion to the stable boy she tossed the dark mane to one side and the sunlight shone on it. She smiled and touched the boy's arm, and they shared a joke that made her laugh out loud. Cherry red lips. Pale skin with just a touch of dusky rose on her cheeks. Sparkling violet eyes. A living swirl of clichés. So free. So *care*free.

The queen's mouth tightened. 'She shouldn't ride in the forest so early. It isn't safe. And she shouldn't ride anywhere dressed like a common boy.'

'Everyone in the kingdom knows who Snow is,' the king said. 'No one would dare harm her. No one would want to. She's like her mother; everyone loves her.'

There was no reproach in his voice. The barb was unintended but it stung all the same. The saintly dead wife.

The glorified beautiful daughter. The queen's mouth twisted slightly. 'She should be thinking about marriage. Finding a decent match for the kingdom.'

Below, Snow White slapped the horse affectionately on the rear as the boy led him away, and then turned to head into the castle. With the sudden awareness a mouse might get as an owl swoops above it she glanced up, her eyes meeting her step-mother's. Her smile wavered nervously for a second and then she raised her hand in a gesture of hello. The queen did not return it. Snow White dropped her hand.

How did she look from down there, the queen wondered. Did her own blonde hair shine in the sunlight? Or was she merely a resentful ghost – a shadow against the glass? She clenched her delicate jaw. The girl disappeared from view but still the queen's teeth remained gritted. They couldn't both stay in this castle for much longer. She couldn't stand it. She stayed where she was, gazing out of the window, and after a few moments the king came and stood behind her.

'It's still early,' he said, his thick body pressed hard against her back. He wrapped his arms around her waist and pulled her closer before one hand slid between the ribbons of her nightdress, seeking out her breast. His fingers were rough against her soft skin; a soldier's touch. She let him caress her.

'We should go back to bed,' he whispered hot in her ear. 'You know I go to war again tomorrow.' He pulled her back from the window, one hand inside her clothes as the other tugged at the bows that held it together. 'Show me how much you'll miss me.'

Finally, she turned away from the window and faced him. His eyes were glazed already and that made her smile. It took so very little from her to make him this way. His dead wife might have been well loved, but she had never had this power. She had never realised her husband was a glutton for everything, or that all men wanted more than just good food on the table and excitement on the battlefield. They wanted excitement in the bedroom too.

She pushed the king back onto the bed and then finished the work he'd started on her shift. It slipped to the floor and she stood naked before him. She smiled and stepped forward, brushing his lips with hers, teasing him, before lowering onto her knees. She met his gaze – hers wanton and challenging, his powerless and full of need. The knot in her stomach unfurled. He was her puppet. His dead wife might have been loved more than she, but love was irrelevant. She didn't care how much he loved her, it was more important that he *wanted* her. And as much as his attentions were rough and coarse, she had learned how to please him beyond any other he had ever had, her dead predecessor included. He called her his water witch – because if there had ever been a lady of the Lake then she must have looked like her, his new queen who had so enchanted him. And even though he was old enough to be her father, she understood the power that gave her. Men were base. They were manageable. The king was her puppet and she would keep it that way. She hardened her heart and ran her slim fingers across his thighs so her red nails scored his skin slightly.

He flinched. She leaned forward and teased the tip of him with her tongue.

'You are so beautiful,' the king murmured.

Yes, the queen thought. Yes, I am. Snow White's face rose unbidden in her mind, and she pushed it angrily away as she took him in her mouth.

The king and his men left the next day in a glorious parade of pomp and ceremony. The queen watched from the battlements as he went off to wage his war against the neighbouring kingdoms. Although it was summer rain fell in a fine mist. Courtiers said that the sky was crying to see their king leave and risk his life for their safety and their kingdom's strength. Lilith, the queen, his water witch, knew better. Rain was just rain, and the king fought for his own ambition, not for his kingdom. It was the one quality she liked about him. The one she could understand.

As the gates opened, he turned and waved up at her and she nodded her farewell, the eyes of the city beyond straining to see her. They waited for her to cry, to show some emotion from behind her icy beauty, but she would not oblige them. She was a queen. She did not perform for the populace. They did not matter to her; they weren't *her* people.

A cheer went up, and the crowd turned their collective gaze from her as if she had been but a momentary distraction. The king's horse stopped as a figure ran towards it; a girl in blue, holding up her dress so the hems didn't get ruined, but still running with the joy of a child who has yet to be corseted instead of cosseted. Snow White. Of course. Above them all the grey sky broke and a shaft of sunlight struck the castle and its grounds. Where the common people had looked at Lilith with wary fascination, they looked upon the father and daughter – especially the daughter – with fondness and love.

The queen kept her chin high. Her spine was straight from the tight stays that bound her, but it stiffened further at the crude display of emotion taking place below. Snow White reached up on her tip toes as her father leaned forward and she threw her arm around his neck, before handing him something she'd held behind her back. An apple. A bright red, perfect apple, the waxy skin catching the sudden light. The crowd cheered again as the king took the fruit, his face splitting into an enormous grin. Snow White stepped back and then curtseyed, her head bowed; once again the dutiful daughter and princess. The people went wild. Snow White, the queen of their hearts. The girl who could wow them all with something as simple as an apple. Everything was so easy for beautiful, lovable, perfect Snow White.

Lilith did not wait for the gates to close behind her husband, but turned and stormed haughtily back into the castle. The king was gone. The last time he had gone to war she had been a young bride, but now she was a woman. A queen. She was in charge and this time she'd make sure her presence was felt.

The drizzle developed into a storm and the whole castle was enveloped in a gloomy hush. The queen did not go to the formal banqueting room for dinner, but instead had a small supper sent to her room. She waited until the last minute, knowing that the cooks would have prepared several roasted meats and delicacies for her to choose from, before she sent a servant to fetch only bread and cheese and wine. The cooks would moan about the waste in a way they never would if the king did the same, but none would do it to her face and that was all that mattered. The king would be gone a long time and the sooner they learned to do as they were told the better. She had been forced to this kingdom and her marriage much against her will but she was learning to make the best of it. Her life could have been much worse. Waiting for her bath to be filled, she gazed out at the rain and the distant glow of the foundries and the mines where the dwarves laboured. Each team worked long shifts and the fires never went out. This was a hardy land and the dwarves were the hardiest of its peoples. She wondered sometimes if they were hardy simply from years spent breaking their backs at the rock face, but when she'd mentioned it to the king he'd grown angry. He'd said that the dwarves enjoyed their work. Hadn't she heard them singing? Her words had stung him – he didn't like to be seen as unkind, even by her.

She had kept her thoughts to herself after that, but she could remember men who sang from the land of her own birth. Those men had been captured in foreign lands and brought across the seas, their dark skin so different from the milky cream of her own, and they too had sung as they'd been forced to beat at the earth and dig fresh roads. Sometimes a song was all a people had.

In its way the king's reaction, however, had amused her. What was this need to be seen as benevolent? If you were going to be cruel, then admit it. Embrace it. Anything else was just self delusion and weakness.

The clatter of horse's hooves sung out above the rain and she opened the window to peer out into the evening. The rain was cold on her face and she squinted against it. The slim, cloaked figure on the horse was holding a heavily laden basket, and a wisp of dark hair was blowing free in the wind.

'I've changed my mind,' the queen said haughtily. 'I'd like my dinner now.'

The cooks and scullery maids kept their heads down. She

could see their skin flushing from the rarity of this visit. She was the queen. She did not venture to the kitchens.

'All of it. I know the courses and I expect to see them all here.' Her words were greeted with silence. Outside, thunder rumbled. She walked carefully along the kitchen table where the platters from the dining room had been laid out. 'And yet they are not. Where is the pigeon? And the venison? There is always a haunch.' Her words were as sharp as the diamonds that covered her, shards of ice filling the air. 'Has one of you stolen it?'

'No, your Majesty.' Finally, the head cook, a fat ageing woman with warts on her chin and yet the softness of expression that told stories of a long and happy marriage and children at her ankles, spoke up. 'You know we would not do that.'

Lilith heard the slight reproach in her voice. As if she were talking to a spoilt child, rather than her queen.

'Then who did?'

'The princess. She said it was a shame for it all to go to waste. She said there were plenty that were in need of such a feast.'

'Who exactly?' Her stomach twisted in a knot of cold snakes as it so often did when the girl was mentioned, but she remained cool. She was practised at it. 'My husband is a generous king. To say otherwise is treason.'

The servants' heads dipped lower, suddenly aware that

they had inadvertently trodden on dangerous ground, but the cook simply twitched an eyebrow.

'The dwarves, your Majesty. She took the food to the dwarves. They've been working through the storm. She's very fond of them.'

'Why was she in the kitchens at all?' The queen continued to move around the table, one slim pale hand poking and touching the dishes, spoiling them for whoever in the room might have thought to eat them for supper. 'This is no place for the royal family.'

'She's always come in here,' the cook said. 'Ever since she was small and the good queen passed away.'

The *good* queen. The word didn't escape her.

'She needed some love,' the cook continued. 'It didn't do her no harm.'

'That's debatable.' Her smile was a razor slash. 'She hardly behaves as a lady of her standing should. I fear your interference has spoiled her.' She drew herself up tall. 'She will not come in here again. If she does, I shall throw whichever of you condones it into the dungeons. You know the kind of creatures we keep down there. You would not last long.'

'The king would not—'

'The king isn't here,' Lilith cut her off. 'And I doubt he'd be impressed at his fine dinners being given to the dwarves. He won't be here for a long time, so you will do as I command.'

She turned to leave, her heavy dress scratching at the floor. 'Oh, and one more thing.' Her cold eyes rested on the cook. 'You are dismissed. Get your things and leave the castle by morning. I will not have you here again.'

The gasps that rippled around the room were satisfaction enough, as was the expression on the woman's face, her mouth and eyes wide in disbelief as if she'd suddenly been slapped hard. In a way she had.

'And count yourself lucky,' the queen added. 'You've all heard the rumours about me. How I enchanted the king? How he calls me his witch? There is magic in my blood and you all know it. I have been kind, old woman. I could have turned you into a crone.'

She did not wait for their reaction but strode away from the suffocating warmth at the heart of the castle. She might not have their love. But she would have their fear.

The only place the queen truly relaxed was in the hidden room she had claimed for her own ever since she arrived. It was in the West Wing of the castle, the side that rarely caught the light and had therefore been mainly abandoned. The servants moved like ghosts through the rooms polishing the floors and ensuring everything sparkled regardless whether any but the queen ever visited.

Her sanctuary was at the back of the great library, a

vast and beautiful domed room filled with row upon row of dusty books that held every story and history of this land, some true, some simply believed to be true, some that had somehow become truth as the years had passed. When they had first married the king had intended to clear the library out and turn it into a winter ballroom. What was the point of it? She had persuaded him otherwise. He had always found it hard to resist her persuasion, and when the day came that he could, then she would resort to other means to keep his interest. The rumours aside, she hadn't needed to enchant him *yet*.

Her secret room had no windows but she didn't mind that, preferring the softer light from candles and lamps as they danced on her treasures. She took a long swallow of red wine and leaned back in her chair, letting her fine blonde hair run down the mahogany back like a waterfall. Tatters of fabric were scattered across the floor and she viewed them with satisfaction. That was one mess she'd have to clean up herself. No servants were allowed in here.

Her gaze grazed the sparkling glass cabinets that housed her possessions. Some she had brought with her on her reluctant journey into marriage, others she had purchased surreptitiously, her nose always checking the wind for the scent of magic, but of late most had come from the boy she sent to search them out. Soon he'd be back again. What would he have found this time? As her great-grandmother had taught her, a wise woman could never have enough magic.

She got to her feet and tugged her black robe tighter, moving through the room and taking comfort from the items and bottled potions and poisons. It wasn't enough to own them, you had to know how and when to use them. More than that, you had to be *prepared* to use them. Her face was reflected in the glass like a ghost on water; fascinating and untouchable. She was beautiful. She had always been the most beautiful woman wherever she was. Ethereal, that's what they called her, both in her own lands and in this new one which she had been forced to take as her home.

Her mother had the same beauty and it was perhaps only that which had saved them both from burning when her father had discovered that they were cuckoos in the royal nest. When he'd found out about her great-grandmother in the woods, the crone in her candy house, where Lilith had spent childhood days learning the craft and playing with the bones of lost children. When he'd realised a witch's curse ran through their blood, he'd locked them both away for days. But her mother was no fool. She'd used her beauty against him. Lilith had been banished into marriage and her father, the king, had declared that cottage and part of the forest out of bounds. Men would do a lot for beauty, that's what Lilith learned in that time. Beauty had a magic all of its own.

'I know you're in there!' The words were accompanied by a pummelling fist on the door. The queen jumped, her reverie broken. She looked down at the mess on the floor again.

Snow White.

'I know you're in there! Open the door!'

How did she know about this room? No one knew about this room! The king might have, once, but he'd have long ago forgotten. His interest in his wife didn't extend very far. She stared at the thick wood and remained silent. The fists beat out another angry round on the other side.

'You fired Maddy! You sent her home! I'm not going anywhere until you open this door. I'll wait until you come out. You can't hide from me forever!'

The queen heard the first hint of tears in the girl's voice, and only then did she pull back the bolts that separated them. She stood in the doorway blocking her possessions from view. Not that it mattered. All of Snow White's attention was on her step-mother. Tears spilled from her eyes, but her skin wasn't blotchy. Her thick dark hair was like a wild mane around her shoulders. If Lilith's beauty was ethereal then Snow's was earthy. Raw and sensual. Standing there, anger and upset making her whole body tremble while her eyes were wild and full of rage, Lilith thought Snow had taken on the spirit of one of the magnificent horses she so loved to ride.

But horses were breakable. They *had* to be broken. That was the way of things. Snow White would be no different in the end.

Lilith remained impassive, a wall of cool ice before the pacing animal. Air and earth. Light and dark.

'What are you doing here?' she asked, eventually, pleased with the mild irritation in her tone. 'This is a private place.'

'This is where you hide,' Snow said. 'I've known about it for ages. Why did you fire Maddy? She's been here since I was a child. You can't fire her; you just can't! I took the food to the forest, not her. It's my fault. If anyone should be punished it's me. And I'm really sorry. I didn't mean to upset you.' She paused. 'I never mean to upset you, although I seem to do it all the time.'

Now that they were face to face, her fire was dying. Snow White had never learned to harness her anger as Lilith had. The queen had watched her over the past three years, since marriage had made them family. The girl was quick to anger, just as quick to forget. Always thinking the best of people. Always wanting everyone to be happy. There were only four years between them but it felt like a lifetime. Lilith was a woman. She'd had to grow up fast. Snow White? She was still a foolish girl.

'She was insolent,' the queen said. 'Not that I have to explain myself to you.'

'You can't dismiss her. My father would hate it.'

Lilith raised an eyebrow and smiled slightly. 'Your father isn't here. I think you'll find I'm in charge. And as for your punishment,' she swung the door open slightly revealing the scraps of cloth on the floor, 'you will no longer go out riding in breeches.'

Snow White's perfect mouth dropped open. 'You cut up my clothes?' Her voice had softened. The anger was fading into something else. 'Why would you do something like that?'

'It's time for you to stop behaving like a child. This will be better for you in the long run. You can't be wild forever, the world won't let you. It doesn't work like that. Trust me.'

'Trust you?' The tears were flowing free now, clear warm streams on the gentle curves of her face. 'Why should I trust you? You hate me! I don't even know why you hate me!' Snow's hands had balled into fists of frustration, and it seemed as if even the dust on the books that surrounded them scuttled away to hide from her anger. 'Are you jealous that my father loves me so much, is that it? Do you want him all for yourself?'

The queen was so surprised she burst into a fit of unexpected laughter. She saw it hit Snow like a punch. Laughter didn't come easily to Lilith – her great-grandmother had taught her to hide her emotions where possible – and she doubted she'd had a belly laugh like this in all the three years of her marriage.

'Oh, that's priceless,' she wiped a tear from her own eye, a laughing mockery of Snow's own, 'truly, it is.' She gasped again as another wave of giggles threatened to overwhelm her. Snow was so wrong it was funny. She thought of the children's bones her great-grandmother used to rap her knuckles with, took two deep breaths to contain her laughter and let the icy mantle that shielded her from the world settle over her once more.

'I don't love your father,' she whispered, the sound somewhere between a hiss and a snarl. 'I loathe him. He repulses me. He's a stupid, fat, arrogant man.' She stepped forward; a precise deadly movement. Snow White didn't move.

'You can't mean that. You can't. You *married* him.'

'You foolish spoilt little princess. Is that what you think? It's all about *true love*? Love and marriage have nothing to do with each other.'

'But he loves you,' Snow said. 'He always says he loves you.'

'He wants me. That's different.' Lilith smiled. 'And I want his power. Men take it so much for granted. You need to learn that the only way to wield it in the kingdoms is by making a great match.' She leaned forward slightly. 'Now he's gone to war and I have it. I will train you to be a lady. I will find you a husband. Then you'll be gone from here and I will have some *peace*.' She spat the last words out before turning back into her room. She slammed the door in the dark beauty's face and shot the bolts across.

Beneath her milky complexion her face was burning and she rested her forehead against the cool wood for a moment. Only the sound of her own ragged breath filled her ears. No fists beat from the other side. Eventually, she straightened up and poured another glass of wine. Snow White had gone. No doubt crying on her bed already, mourning her dead mother and wishing her father had never married again.

The candlelight was softly comforting and she lost herself in its dance on the crimson surface. Her thoughts were as dark as the liquid she swirled in the glass and she was drowning in them, the here and now forgotten. In the corner, hidden in the shadows, a black cabinet hung on the wall. The imp who'd sold it to her, long ago, had said it was made from the bones of burned saints from the barbaric lands across the sea, that the glass the cabinet housed came from the blood of mermaids, and the magic bound in it came from the Far Mountain itself.

For a long while she'd tried to ignore it. As the door creaked open, she took a deep drink from the glass. Her head would hurt in the morning.

'She truly is the fairest in the land.'

Lilith looked up. She saw the familiar face in the glass, hung on the inside of the door, was surrounded by inlaid precious jewels. The emeralds sparkled green.

'Shut up,' she said.

She should have smashed that mirror. It had belonged to an emperor in the East, the imp claimed, stolen as he lay dying after a hundred year reign. The story went that he had opened the cabinet every day for every one of those years and listened to its words. She didn't believe it. The lands were filled with stories, most of which were just inventions. She didn't think anyone could bear the enchanted mirror day after day.

'*And so graceful.*' In the mirror the face was frozen but the words came anyway, from some end less place behind the glass that could never be under stood. It was a soft voice full of warmth, but still every syllable stung the queen. Her jaw tightened.

'I said, shut up.'

'*Everyone loves her, don't they? And it's so easy to see why. Beauty and kindness and yet still wild and free. She will have her pick of the princes to fall in love with. Yes, she truly is the fairest in the land. Isn't she? Isn't she beautiful?*'

Cold, bitter fire burned in the queen's heart and it erupted in a screech as she launched her goblet at the glass. The door slammed shut and the liquid splatted like blood across the gargoyle faces which decorated it. She stared as it trickled across their open eyes and dripped to the floor.

'Good,' she hissed. 'If she wants a prince then I shall find her one. One who will take her far, far away.'

She trembled and magic tingled on her skin. She spun round, leaving the spilt wine to drip red over the shredded fabric, the wind from her robe snuffing out the candle, and she stormed out into the dark.

One way or another, Snow White had to go.

2

'A giant from the Far Mountains'

By the time the king had been gone a month, things had changed significantly in the castle and the land beyond. It was astounding how much could be done in so short a time when you put your mind to it. The king, although bluff enough by nature and deed, had never given much thought to his subjects who lived beyond the castle walls. They loved him, they always had, and they paid their taxes which allowed him to go on his wars. In turn he made sure they had enough food to be the right side of starving, but not too much that they would become greedy and consider rebellion. The king took them for granted, in a way that only one born to a throne really can. They got on with their business and he got on with his and they cheered when he passed on his horse and that was generally enough.

There were no statues or portraits of him in public places. He hadn't seen the need. Having narrowly escaped the flames in the land of her birth, the queen, more than most, understood the power of public perception. She did not have their love or their natural fealty, but she knew how to get their fear and respect.

She wanted the people to feel she was watching them at all times. The busts and paintings in every hall and market took care of that, along with, for a brief time at least, a network of spies who ensured she knew enough to make the people believe that she could see all of their secrets. She dealt a very visible and unpleasant justice to a few merchants who had been less than honest with their taxes, and the rumours of the queen's sharp eye and iron grip subsequently spread like fire through the kingdom. Her spies added a few stories of dark magic and soon all cheered loudly when she passed but none would meet her eyes.

People were so easy.

Life in the castle had changed as well, especially for Snow White. The stable boys had been ordered to saddle only the gentle mares should she wish to ride, and she'd been instructed – under pain of punishment falling on her maids – to dress according to her station at all times. The queen had ordered a selection of dresses to be sent from her own kingdom for her step-daughter. They came with stiffer corsets and stronger binding than they made here, and if she wore them for a month or two she'd realise what a blessing her normal dresses were. Perhaps then she wouldn't fight wearing them so much. Maybe then she'd see there was no point in fighting any of it.

On top of this, Snow White was no longer allowed to find refuge in the servants' quarters, and although she still roamed the forest – even the queen could not imprison her in the castle – and visited her beloved dwarves out by the mines, her visits were less frequent and always reported. A little magic here, a curse here and there, was all it took to gain the loyalty of the forest folk. Her great-grandmother had taught her well.

No one would dare defy the queen's orders, however much they hated seeing their beloved princess so unhappy. And she was *desperately* unhappy but that, after all, the queen reminded herself, was the point. Why would Snow White agree to a marriage if she was happy at home? The queen wanted her gone. She *needed* her gone. And if there was one thing she'd learned in her lifetime it was that nothing was ever achieved without a little pain.

She swept out into the busy courtyard her black dress, glittering with precious black rubies that dwarves had died to find, at odds with the brightly coloured ribbons and bunting that were being hung from the walls and posts. Doves cooed in boxes. Merchants dragged carts filled with all manner of foods and the finest wines towards the heavy doors that led to the store rooms and kitchens. The preparations were well under way. Even though she prided herself on quelling her emotions, Lilith felt a small tingle of excitement run through her veins. By the following evening her plans would have come to fruition.

It was the queen's twenty-fourth birthday and she was having the most magnificent ball. All the finest ladies and gentlemen of the city would be there and she had invited handsome princes and noblemen from all of the allied kingdoms as well. Her jaw tightened. Snow White would be, as the saying went, like a pig in shit amongst them.

She snapped unnecessary orders and then retreated inside. She kept her head high, ignoring the sharp glances from the women scrubbing the floor. The corridor was one hundred feet long and the two ageing women had reached approximately half way. Their knees would be raw and bruised and no doubt their lower bodies would ache and cramp for the rest of the day when they were done. She'd learned as a child in her great-grandmother's cottage that scrubbing floors could be back-breaking work. She reached the far end and then paused and turned.

'Not good enough,' she said. 'Start again.' This time they did look up, eyes wide in their tired, sagging faces. The queen tightened her lips, accentuating the sharp angles of her delicate beauty, each one like a knife's blade. 'Right from the door.'

She watched as the two women hauled themselves to their feet, picked up their buckets and brushes and hobbled, broken, back to where they had started hours before. They didn't argue and Lilith allowed herself a small smile. The old queen and her daughter had the people's love. She would have their fear. It was a hardier emotion. As she turned away she felt a small twinge in her chest and wondered idly if it was a small part of her own heart turning black and hardening. Good, she thought. The sooner the better.

'Come on,' Snow White said as she wiped her tears of laughter away. 'Let's try again.' She took a sip from the beer tankard, sighed, hitched out another laugh, and then passed the mug along to the first of the dwarves who were picking themselves up on the grass.

'It's never going to work,' Dreamy said. 'And I'm not sure the beer is helping.' He was sitting beside the princess on the wooden table, having taken and caused enough bruises during the previous attempts to get himself removed from the proceedings for all their safety.

'Beer helps everything.' She winked. 'It will relax them.' She clapped and laughed. 'Try again. Grouchy, you on the bottom. I think you're the hardiest!'

There were exclamations of protest as each of the dwarves wanted to be the strongest in Snow White's eyes, even though they knew in their hearts that she loved them all equally. Grouchy, squinting in the warm sunshine, steadied himself and then Feisty clambered onto his shoulders. When he was steady the next climbed the rickety ladder to perch on his shoulders.

'Keep going! It's amazing!' Snow White said, smiling. 'We can do this! You can do this!'

'It'll go wrong at the top. It's the coat. It unbalances them.' Dreamy took a swallow of beer from the mug.

'Hmmm,' Snow White frowned, looking at Bolshy, drowning in the overcoat designed to cover them all and with his shoulders padded out with quilted coat hangers to make him ridiculously broad. 'You might have a point. Maybe Grouchy needs to be at the top.'

A few moments, and another tumble to the grass later and she was proved right. Luckily although the dwarves weren't good at balancing, they were good at landing. The mines weren't safe and tunnels often gave way, dropping them great heights to the rocks below. If they didn't know how to land, they didn't live long. The grass might as well have been cushions for what they were used to and so after more giggles, more beer and a dusting down, they began again, this time with Grouchy draped in the coat and going up last.

'Are you sure this is a good idea?' Dreamy asked. He'd been wondering it for a while, but had been caught up in the fun of it with the rest of them, and when Snow White was enthusiastic about something it was hard not to get swept along. But now that he was sitting out and watching, doubts niggled at him.

'What do you mean? It'll be funny.'

'I'm sure it *could* be funny,' he said, slightly hesitant. 'But I'm not sure your step-mother has a sense of humour.'

'That's where you're wrong.' Snow White smiled and squeezed his knee. 'She used to have one. When she first got here. I remember we used to laugh a lot. She laughed yesterday.' She looked away from him. 'She's just lost her reasons to have fun, that's all. Maybe that's what being married does to you.' Snow took the mug from Dreamy. 'I'm getting it now. She just doesn't like being married very much. And that must make someone quite unhappy.'

'She's not unhappy,' Dreamy muttered. 'She's plain mean.'

'Well, maybe unhappiness makes people mean.' Her eyes sparkled as she looked at the tower of small men which looked like it might actually stay together for more than thirty seconds. 'But my father's gone to war again, for a long time this time, I think, so we need to make her smile. It's her birthday, she'll love it.'

'You think too well of people, Snow White.'

'Someone's got to, Dreamy.'

The precarious tower took a few hesitant steps towards her.

'Yes!' Snow White leapt from the table and almost jumped with glee. 'We've got it! You've done it!' She looked over her shoulder at Dreamy, her grin enticing and wicked. 'This is going to be amazing!'

* * *

It was a magnificent affair. The chandeliers sparkled and filled the vast space with light. Musicians in every corner created a magical symphony in perfect time with each other although so far apart. Masked servants circled the room with platters of the most exquisite canapés and wines each served at their perfect temperature. Every invited guest was in attendance, and the gowns worn by the ladies transformed even the plainest of them.

The queen surveyed the room from her throne. It was a sea of pastel colours, as was the tradition of such events. She'd chosen to wear red, the same colour on her lips. Even those who hated her, and their number was growing fast, had to admire her beauty. Her blonde hair hung long and straight down her back, the colour of the far off winter lands. And her heart, she'd heard them whispering, was just as hard.

She smiled but she did not join them, although she commanded the music and watched the timeless dance between the sexes begin. A glance that lingered too long. A smile behind a fan. Eyes that peeked up playfully from a bow. It was always the same. She wondered how many ever ended happily ever after? Her mother had wanted that. It hadn't lasted.

After the first round of dancing came the entertainment as her guests ate and drank some more. There were the tumblers, the piper and his dancing rats, the fire eaters and the dancers, and soon the music would begin again. The queen clenched her teeth. The ball was in full swing and Snow White had yet to appear. She snapped her fingers. A footman scurried over and bowed.

'Send someone to the princess's rooms. Tell her she must come at once. I will not have her keeping my guests waiting longer.' Enough was enough. There was lateness and then there was arrogance. 'This delay is clearly the fault of her maids.' Lilith smiled. 'Make sure the princess knows that I shall punish them for embarrassing her if she does not arrive within five minutes.' She gestured for music, sat as far back in her throne as the stiff upright chair would allow and focused on her annoyance rather than how easily the threats came from her these days, or on the knowledge that she would follow through on them if she had to.

The footman, however, had barely turned to leave when the trumpet sounded and the doors at the far end opened wide. The orchestras stopped, trickling away to nothing as the performers forgot their notes and their bows hung in mid air above the strings. Even the queen was breathless for a second at the sight of Snow White's beauty. Gasps punctuated the stillness. Snow White stepped through the doors and paused at the top of the three marble steps that led down to the ballroom. She wore a pure white dress, strapless and fitted, so different to the full skirted style that the ladies of the court preferred, and it was decorated with small purple jewels. The same gems sparkled in her dark hair, swept high and tousled on her head, and they served to highlight the violet of her eyes.

All attention on her, she smiled and curtseyed, a more sensuous movement than all the years of training had ever given Lilith. The queen dragged her eyes away from the beautiful girl and got to her feet, scanning the ballroom. Every prince was staring, their pretty dancing partners completely forgotten, as if they were simply shadows. Snow White could have her pick of them, that was clear. A shard of envy pierced her hardening heart, and her face ached with the effort of maintaining her smile. Still. That didn't matter. Snow White would be gone, out of the kingdom forever, and then maybe she would be able to relax.

'I'm so sorry I'm late,' Snow said, addressing the room. If Lilith was ice then Snow White was warm honey, and the mischievous twinkle as she smiled only enhanced her beauty. 'But I was waiting for my companion.' She held out one hand and curtseyed again as a man, thus far out of sight, came through the open doorway and joined her on the steps.

The queen, always so controlled, could not contain her gasp. He stood eight feet or more tall and wore a bright purple suit with a silver trim, the colour almost an exact match to the gems adorning the princess. A painted mask covered most of his face.

'May I introduce Agard, Prince of the Far Mountains, home of the Giants.' She smiled again and took the enormous man's hand, leading him into the party. Dresses rustled as men and women pulled away from them creating a path, not entirely out of politeness. The queen wasn't the only one who was shocked. No one had been near the Far Mountains for as long as she'd been alive, and probably not in the generation before either. How could Snow possibly have...?

'We've been communicating by dove since I found one injured in the forest with a message attached to its leg and restored it to health. The prince wanted to reach out to distant people, and he found me.'

The strange couple moved further and further into the room, taking remarkably short steps given the man's height, the queen noticed. Was he compensating for Snow White? How could he possibly have got into the castle without one of her spies telling her? And how could she have possibly fallen in love with this giant, as it seemed clear she had?

Her eyes fixed on their progress, Lilith tried to relax. It didn't matter which man Snow White chose. In fact, this creature might be a blessing in disguise. The king would surely disapprove of their union – what monstrous children would they create, for one thing? – and it was unlikely that Snow White would ever be allowed to return from the Far Mountains. The girl was embarrassing herself, but she was also doing all of Lilith's work for her. She needn't have wasted time and money inviting all the princes to a grand ball. Perhaps she should have just called for a circus or a freak show and given her step daughter more to choose from.

As they approached, she walked forward to meet them and then curtseyed deeply at the giant's feet. Snow's curtsey might have been sensuous but the queen's was elegant and flawless, her back remaining perfectly straight. She made the gesture seem so effortless, but hours of training and tears had gone into it when she was four years old. The backs of her knees had been bruised and bleeding from the thwacks of the ruler her instructress used to inflict if she didn't do it perfectly. Her father, the king, would not accept less than a perfect princess for a daughter. She had become one for him, despite herself. Even if magic ran in her veins as well as royal blood. It was a man's world and she had learned to play the game. What else could a woman with beauty and brains do?

'Your highness,' the queen said. 'Welcome to our home. We are honoured to be the first of the kingdoms to receive a visit from the people of the Far Mountains, and I hope it shall not be your last. We have heard so much of your strength and generosity of spirit.' Her words were clear and humble although most of what she'd heard of the giants was that they were clumsy, stupid and greedy and spent most of their time fighting each other. Legend said that whenever rocks fell in the low lands, a giant in the Far Mountains was stamping his feet because he couldn't get his own way. But she was a queen and she would behave like one.

'Thank you, your Majesty.' The giant's voice was gruff but not as resonant as she expected. But then what did she really know of them? Nothing. Their guest began to lean forward to bow. The movement started well and then suddenly he wobbled, losing his balance and tilting dangerously sideways. The queen stepped backwards as two courtiers rushed forward and took the giant's hands to stabilise him.

It was only then the queen noticed how small the hand was. How could a giant...?

Before she could finish her thought, the giant's middle section began to erupt. Buttons flew from the purple suit. Somewhere amongst the guests an idiot girl shrieked and another fainted. From within the giant came several exclamations before the body finally collapsed into a small pile of moving pieces.

For a moment there was silence and then Snow White burst into warm laughter. 'I knew they couldn't balance for long, but I was hoping for a first dance at least.' She turned to the assembled guests. 'A giant from the Far Mountains? Oh, come, come. You really fell for that? Anyway, my companions are far more impressive than any giant.'

The bundle of dwarves slowly pulled themselves to their feet. Lilith stepped backwards, icy cold anger running through her pumping heart. She had curtseyed to them, these strange rough mining men. She had addressed them as royals, and worse than all of that was that they had tricked her.

The little men lined up alongside Snow White and bowed. The gathered guests laughed and applauded as did Snow herself. They blushed and muttered to each other, but their bashful joy at being part of this humiliating game was obvious. Snow White leaned down and kissed their heads and two of the little faces turned almost the colour of their princess's jewels.

Snow stood alongside the queen and faced the guests. 'It is so lovely to see so many visitors from other kingdoms here,' she nodded and smiled at several of the princes. 'Some of you I have not seen since childhood when I would beat you all to the top of the trees.' Again, there was a round of laughter. Black crept into the corner of Lilith's vision as she raged inside. This was uncalled for. Women did not make speeches at balls. Even she hadn't and the purpose of the occasion was *her* birthday. Kings and princes made speeches. That was the protocol in all the allied kingdoms. What was Snow White doing? Why were all the guests so enamoured of her that they didn't care? Why was it all so *easy* for her?

'I am so very fond of you all,' Snow White continued, apparently unaware of the waves of hatred coming from the slim figure in red beside her. 'But if you have come here to seek my hand in marriage, then let me put you at ease so we can all just enjoy this wonderful party. I have no desire to be betrothed to any of you. You will not find marriage with me.' She raised a dark eyebrow. 'Although perhaps you might with some of the lovely ladies you're already dancing with.' Around the room couples blushed and moved closer together. Lilith felt sick, the few morsels of food she'd eaten curdling in her stomach. The princess was making a fool of her. Was she supposed to just smile through this embarrassment? Was she doing it on purpose... some act of revenge in front of princes from all the kingdoms?

'You are all handsome and charming men,' Snow White continued. 'But I will only ever surrender myself to true love.' She glanced at the queen and smiled, and from behind her own smile all Lilith wanted to do was choke the triumphant expression from the girl's face.

'Until then,' Snow finished, 'I shall make do with the company of my friends.' She looked down once again at the dwarves who bowed in unison, first to Snow White, then to the queen and then to the guests, who gave another round of spontaneous applause.

The musicians returned their bows to their instruments and the air was filled with music. The party began again, but this time there was a belle for their ball; the wonderful, unique Snow White. She led the dancing with the princes and the dwarves, so unlike the icy queen who oversaw the revelry from her throne. Within fifteen minutes Lilith, for all her great beauty, had been forgotten and she gladly slipped away, forcing herself to maintain a steady pace instead of bursting into a run as soon as she was through the doors.

The corridor echoed with laughter that chased her until she was sure she was the cause of it. They were all laughing at her. Of course they were. She fled through the castle, a whirlwind of blazing fury, until at last there was only the silence of her forgotten library and the dry books which were as unloved as she was. Her pace slowed but still books fell from the shelves as she passed, her rage and hurt slamming them to the ground.

Finally, there was the comfort of the room beyond. Her room. Her things. Her power was here. Her honesty was here. This was who she was. The candles and lamps lit as she glanced at them. Her magic was always stronger in anger and high emotion. Her mother's magic had been weak, she hadn't exercised it. Lilith had no intention of that happening to hers. She would no longer be ashamed of it.

She poured warm red wine from the silver decanter that never emptied, and drank the first glass quickly. Her hand was still trembling when she poured the second. Her eyes were glittering diamonds in the candlelight. How could they have humiliated her like that? How could she have let them? Her insides twisted; a ball of snakes trapped by the fires of her emotions. She wanted to cry. She wanted to scream. She wanted to shout at the girl and shake her until she understood that the world *expected* things of her.

Behind glass, her crystal ball glowed red and green and then a rainbow of colours. With her glass refilled she sat in her chair and stared at it, letting the colours entrance and calm her. She drank quickly until her vision was hazy and her angry thoughts could no longer keep their sharp edges, and then she put the goblet down. She allowed herself to be lost in the colours and her memories of the past. Of happier times. Of being free.

'Why did you leave?'

The words, cutting the silence, made her jump and she turned to see the door open and Snow White, in all her beautiful finery, standing at the threshold. In her anger she hadn't locked herself in. She cursed under her breath.

'It's your birthday ball. You should be there.'

The queen rose to her feet, happy to find her legs steady. It took more than a heady wine to take her steel.

'You humiliated me,' she hissed. 'And at my own birthday. I suppose you thought that was funny.'

'It was supposed to be a joke,' Snow White said, her eyes wide with innocence and hurt. 'I thought you'd like it. I thought you'd *get* it.'

Lilith wondered how much practice went into that look. The king and the courtiers might be fooled by it, but the queen would not be.

'So, now you're calling me stupid? A little girl like you

who wants to play with dwarves thinks she can laugh at me?' Where the candlelight accentuated each of Snow's soft curves and full features, the queen knew it hardened her sharp cheekbones and cast shadows under her eyes. She wondered how she must look. Still the great beauty of the North, or a harpy? She found she did not much care. 'Or do you really want to marry one? Maybe you'd like to marry all seven of your friends? It could be arranged. They'd tire you out soon enough.'

'Why do you have to be so horrible?' Snow White reeled slightly, and stepped backwards. 'What happened to you? Why must you always be so mean?'

Lilith opened her mouth to laugh and then Snow White's gaze shifted from her to something behind them in the dark shadows of the room. The familiar creak of the cabinet. The queen's eyes widened.

'*She is so beautiful. Snow White, the fairest in all the lands.*'

'What is that?' Snow said, curiosity replacing her hurt. 'Have you got someone in here with you? Their voice is... strange.'

'It's nothing.' The queen flashed a look behind her, seeing the mirror glint slightly in the dark. 'Nothing for you to—'

'*None can compare, none shall ever compare, to Snow White.*'

'Is that a talking *cupboard*?' Snow White tried to push

past, but Lilith blocked her way. 'One of your crazy magic things the servants talk about?'

'I said it was—' The queen shoved her backwards.

'*Such a beauty. Such a heart. So easy to love. Snow White. Unbearably beautiful, isn't she?*'

The cabinet slammed shut and silent with the ferocity of the queen's glare.

'It was talking about me,' Snow White said. Her eyes came back to the queen's. '*The fairest in the land.* You have a cupboard that *talks* about me?' She laughed suddenly, a short, shocked burst of emotion. 'What is *wrong* with you?'

'Shut up,' the queen said. 'Shut up and get out.'

'You *are* jealous of me,' Snow said. 'Not of my father loving me, but of everyone else. It's not that hard, you know, to have people like you. You just have to be *nice*.'

'I said get out!' She spat the words at the girl, her fists balled. 'You know nothing. You're stupid and blind and I hate you.'

Snow White's jaw clenched. 'Well, your cabinet doesn't. Maybe I should take it back to the party instead.'

The queen could see the mockery clearly in the princess's eyes. She took a deep breath and drew her self up tall. 'You'll regret this. All of it. I promise you.'

'Look, why can't we—'

'Go back to the party. Enjoy it. Tomorrow your dwarves are banished from the palace grounds. On pain of death.'

'You can't—'

The slamming door cut off the rest of Snow White's shocked sentence, and this time the queen remembered to pull the bolt across. Her breathing filled the room but this time it was slow and calm. A chill bloomed inside her. She looked back at the crystal ball. A black mist swirled inside it. So be it, the queen thought grimly. So be it.

3

'A wish is just a curse in disguise'

The new dresses arrived two days after the ball. The atmosphere had remained frosty, the queen had avoided Snow White and it seemed the princess had been doing the same because it was only now, as they both stood in the princess's rooms, that they were face to face since their argument. That suited Lilith.

'Are you sure they'll fit?' one of Snow White's handmaids said. She was a small, mousy thing who could probably come somewhere close to pretty if she straightened her shoulders and put some curls in her hair but, as things stood, she erred on the side of plain.

'Of course they'll fit,' she said.

'It'll break me in half to wear this,' Snow White had pulled on the blue dress closest to her. 'These bones are criminal. There's no give in them.'

'There isn't supposed to be any. They'll stop you slouching.'

'I want my old clothes back.' Her simmering resentment was clear in the flash of her defiant violet eyes. Lilith had never seen eyes that colour before. She wondered if maybe the girl had magic in her too.

'You had no right to take them.' The dress still undone, Snow White stood with her hands on her hips, her hair falling loose over her shoulders. 'No right at all.'

'I had every right,' Lilith snapped, aware that the two maids had drawn close together and were no doubt memorising every word of this confrontation to take down to the servants' quarters and relay as soon as they could. 'You're twenty years old. You need to be preparing for marriage.'

'I don't want to get married,' Snow White said, looking squarely at her. 'I'm not seeing the appeal.'

Lilith ignored her and, with her teeth gritted, grabbed the laces at the back of the dress. Beneath them, Snow White's skin was white and soft, used to freedom. By tonight, if she did as she was told and stayed in the garment, it would be sore where the bindings had been. The laces shone beautifully but were coarse and rough, woven from looms housed in the attics of castles far away. There was no comfort in the court dresses of her own kingdom. She'd forgotten how unforgiving they were. Still, it would do Snow White good to wear them for a while. To feel what it was like to be so trapped by something that you felt you couldn't breathe.

She pulled tighter, the laces burning her cold fingers like rope, and Snow White gasped.

'Not too tight, your Majesty,' the other maid stepped forward. This one was bolder. Older perhaps, and her eyes met the queen's. 'I can do it.'

'You will stay silent,' Lilith spat, and the girl, whatever bravery she might have had, slunk back a few steps like a scolded cat.

'It is really tight,' Snow White said, her voice small. 'I'm not sure I can breathe properly.'

'That's how it should be.' The stays secured, the queen stepped back. Her fingers flashed white against pink and burned where she'd pulled the laces so tight. 'There. Now you look like a proper princess. Of course you won't be able to ride like that. And if you have hidden some *other* clothes somewhere...' The darting glance from Snow White confirmed that was the case, '... then don't even think about changing into them.'

'I'll ride anyway,' Snow White said. Her faced had paled.

'Don't be so ridiculous,' Lilith said. 'You can't.'

'You can't stop me!' The girl pushed past her and stormed out into the corridor. 'I'll do what I want!'

Lilith stared at the door. There was no way she could go riding, not in that dress. She was just having a tantrum.

Always the child. Always so child-like.

'I'm surprised she hasn't broken a rib,' one of the servants muttered. 'Far too tight.'

Lilith ignored them both and strode out of the room. The boy was due back at any moment and she had more to think about than the disapproval of a pair of foolish maids. Her fingertips still felt numb from working on the rough stays. She thought of Snow White's soft skin that would be rubbed by the bone and pinched by the tightness of the bindings.

Good, she thought bitterly. Good.

The queen was never fooled by Aladdin. He always returned full of simpering smiles and obsequious comments but she knew that, underneath them all, he hated her. No, he *loathed* her. Of course he did. No one ever liked anyone they were beholden to, or who controlled them. That was the nature of people; more than that, Aladdin simply wasn't a very pleasant child. Even by Lilith's standards.

He was standing in front of her, perhaps thirteen years old, as he always would be, wearing the same clothes he wore on any of these trips – the only clothes he could possibly wear, and his dark eyes danced in that Arabian face which was made to be the subject of tales in market places where snakes danced to tunes played by weathered men. He bowed.

She waved him up, but kept her distance. Their whole

relationship was based on a lie, but she felt no guilt about that. After all, Aladdin had murdered a great magician to get the lamp in the first place, and then he'd murdered his own father when he'd tried to sell the lamp. Greed could be a terrible thing, but greed combined with the wickedness of this small boy's heart was a terrible combination.

The boy, however, had never learned the secret of the lamp. The curse of it. How could he have? The genie hadn't been about to tell him and Aladdin was too arrogant to realise that with magic there was always a catch. Ten wishes. That was all you got. Although technically it was nine, because once you breathed your tenth wish the genie was free – and you took their place. You became the slave to the next owner of the lamp. The genie Aladdin had freed had been wise to sell it to her – he'd had enough of magic, and he was perceptive enough to know the boy was a psychopath. When he eventually regained his freedom he would hunt the old genie down. He did not want that sword hanging over his head. Lilith had promised him that while she would make the boy hers to command, she would never make a single wish. It suited her anyway. Her grandmother had taught her early on that a wish was just a curse disguised.

Lilith had used the powers of the lamp more wisely than for wishes and whims. She would let the boy out for two weeks at a time to go and search for magical items for her. He was a slave of the lamp and had to do her bidding. If he returned empty handed then she made the delay before his next release much longer. She had quickly learned that Aladdin did not like being caged. But then, who did? She'd promised him that one day she'd give the lamp to an enemy to make his ten wishes and then the boy would be free. That would never happen. She'd heard the reports of unsettling, sadistic murders that always occurred when he was abroad from the lamp, and she was sure that not even a queen would be safe from him.

The room was as ever lit by flickering candles and as he handed over the small silver comb, it glittered in the glow. Two unicorns were carved into it, their heads bowed at each other. It was a pretty trinket, that was for sure, but in itself it held no interest for her.

'It brings the wearer happiness. Great happiness,' Aladdin said. He smiled, his small teeth white and sharp. He had blood under his fingernails. She didn't want to ask about that.

'Happiness?' she said, sharply. Too sharply. The word had stung her – could he sense her unhappiness? Was that it?

'That is, after all, the only thing some people desire, isn't it?' His dark eyes watched her carefully. 'To be happy?'

She stared at him, trying to read something in his cold, dead eyes. 'Well, then they are fools,' she said eventually and then snapped her fingers and said the word and enjoyed the moment of pain and anger that flashed across his face as the tarnished lamp on the table sucked him back in through the spout.

She looked at the comb again. Happiness. For a moment she was almost tempted to slide it into her blonde hair, but instead she put it in the glass cabinet, before carefully placing the lamp beside it. False happiness was probably no happiness at all.

Snow White was barely breathing when Grouchy and Dreamy found her. Her face was pale and her horse was whinnying and pawing at the ground in distress beside her.

'Can't... breathe...' she finally whispered, her lips almost blue and her violet eyes watery with fear. Dreamy stared at her in horror. Had the horse thrown her? Had she fallen? 'My... dress...'

'Quickly!' Grouchy snapped. 'Get your knife!' He was already rolling the limp girl over and pulling at the cords tied so tightly at her back. Dreamy, with trembling hands, scrabbled at his belt, pulling the small blade free and almost dropping it before Grouchy snatched it away from him, forcing the blade under the rough thick strings and tearing through them. One by one they broke, and Snow White's breath came deep and fast and desperate as she sucked the air into her starved lungs. She coughed and sat up, the dress gaping open at the back to reveal purple bruises in lines across her pale back. Her whole body trembled and she struggled to her feet.

'No,' Dreamy said. 'Sit down.'

'It's fine,' Snow White said, the words more wheeze than sound. 'Really, I'm...'

And with that, she fainted.

The queen knew what they were saying about her. That she'd known Snow White would go riding, if only to spite her, and she'd laced the stays too tight on purpose. That she'd known the exertion would suffocate the princess and she'd die in the forest somewhere.

It had been a day and a half since she'd come back, wrapped in a dwarf blanket, her back and ribs as violet as her eyes with bruising. The queen had tried to apologise but Snow White hadn't even paused, just gone into her rooms and locked the doors. Lilith had questioned her maids of course, and they told her the princess had simply had a long bath and then slept. The queen ordered them to remove all the new dresses and have them burned. She'd supervised their destruction herself. She'd hoped it would go part way to an apology but it had dawned on her, as she caught the looks flashing between the kitchen staff as each of the new garments was thrust into the oven, that they thought she might just be disposing of the evidence.

Her heart thumped hard as she stood in her room of treasures. Her face was flushed. She poured wine with a shaking hand and swallowed half the glass in one go. It was too early to drink but she needed to calm herself. What had she done? The glimpse of the bruises on Snow White's body haunted her. She'd gone too far. How could she take it back? How could she make it better? It was one thing to be feared, and quite another to have the entire castle thinking she'd tried to murder the princess. Had messages been sent to the king already? She needed to get more spies abroad. She needed eyes everywhere.

She drank more wine and tried to breathe deeply, finally calming. There were images she couldn't shift though. The bruises. The glare of the old dwarf who'd defied her ruling to bring the princess back safely. And more than all of that, Snow White's face as she walked past Lilith in the corridor as if she wasn't there. Her eyes watering still. Her shoulders slumped. She'd looked defeated. All her natural fire had gone. She'd looked so desperately unhappy.

Unhappy.

Lilith stared into the glass cabinet, her reflection like a sad watery ghost trapped on the other side. She stared so long her breath misted the surface. But still, on its velvet cushion, the small silver hair comb shone in the candlelight. She'd tried to apologise but just couldn't get the words out. She'd never get the right words out, not now. She thought of the corsets. She thought of her own unhappy marriage and her relief when the king had gone to war again. She tried to imagine Snow White, so wild and free, confined in a marriage like hers. No tight corset could prepare you for that. Her head was giddy with wine and her heart was heavy with things she didn't understand.

In a moment of impetuousness, the kind she hadn't felt since she'd been a child running through the forest around her great-grandmother's house, she grabbed the hair comb from the cabinet and thrust it into a small box. She didn't pause. She didn't hesitate. She didn't want to change her mind. She ran out through the empty library, one hand holding her skirt up while her hair flew out behind her like a bridal train. Maybe she could make things better, after all. Maybe false happiness wouldn't be so bad if the person didn't know. Surely the happiness was all that counted?

By the time she arrived at Snow White's rooms she was flushed and out of breath. It had been a long time since she'd moved with such abandon, and she paused and smoothed her dress and stood tall before opening the door. She could do this. She could apologise.

The two maids were tidying the room and changing the water in the jug on the table. Lilith stared at the large bed that was now neatly made and empty.

'Where's Snow White?' she asked. 'I thought she was recuperating?'

'She's gone out,' the prettier of the two answered. 'Don't worry, she's not gone riding. She's still too bruised for that.'

The barb in the remarks stung but Lilith kept her chin up. She might owe Snow White an apology, but not these girls.

'Where is she?'

'She went walking,' the drab looking thing said, eager not to be entirely outdone by her peer. 'Not sure where though. Maybe to the market.'

Lilith didn't pause. She knew if she hesitated then she'd change her mind and the moment would be lost. She thrust the box at the more confident girl. 'Here. It's a gift for her.'

The servant took it cautiously.

'It's for Snow White alone. No one else is to touch it. Do you understand?' She was glad to hear her voice returning to normal. To the icy cool that had become normal at any rate. 'There will be grave consequences if you disobey me.'

'Yes, your Majesty.' The girl's eyes dropped. She knew her place. 'Of course, your Majesty.'

'Tell her I want...' Lilith stopped and her voice softened, 'Tell her I would like her to wear it to dinner this evening.'

'Yes, your Majesty.'

'Good.' She turned and left them, and she felt better than she had in a long time. Perhaps it was just the wine.

* * *

The girl died two hours later.

She hadn't been pretty to start with but in death her face was left frozen in the agony in which she'd died. No longer mousy and hunched, her body was contorted and her hair matted and red where her scalp had bled from contact with the poison. It was Snow White who had found her, and after the doctors had been called and the body removed from the hushed castle, it was Snow White who now stood trembling with anger, her violet eyes flecked with red from crying, in front of her.

'The comb was poisoned,' she said, eventually, once she'd got her breathing under control. 'It killed Tillie, but it was meant for me. *You* gave it to me. She only tried it on because she wanted to look pretty. Like a princess!'

'It wasn't like that,' Lilith said. Her haughtiness had left her and her stomach was a watery pit of fear. The stays being too tight had been one thing. But this, this to all and sundry, looked like attempted murder. What would the whispers be saying now? How far would they travel? 'I didn't know.'

'You didn't know?' Snow White almost laughed. Her nose was running and she wiped it with the back of her hand. 'You know everything!'

'I thought it was simply enchanted.' Tears pricked at her and she did her best to swallow them down, but one broke free, cutting a sparkling track down the angles of her face. 'That's all. Why would I poison you? And if I wanted to poison you why would I do it so *obviously*?' Her fear was turning to aggression, just as it always had, even when she was a little girl. 'I was *trying* to say sorry.'

'Enchanted?' Snow White stared at her. 'What do you mean?'

'It doesn't matter.' Around them, the unused library had settled into silence as if listening to their story so as to bind it and add it to their shelves later. 'It was supposed to bring you happiness. I almost used it myself.'

'I don't trust your magic,' Snow White said. Her voice was calmer and her eyes, although still hurt, were now confused. It was a gift and a blessing, this trait she had of wanting to believe the best in everyone.

'I didn't know it was poisoned,' Lilith repeated. The dark beauty stared at her for a long time, and the queen knew that if there was ever a moment for all the secrets she hid, this was the time to share them. They choked in her throat, though. She couldn't bring herself to set them free.

'I believe you,' the princess said eventually. 'But stay away from me.' She turned and walked away and didn't look back. The queen didn't blame her, but she also knew that things had changed. How could this be kept a secret? A girl had been killed by her gift and Snow White no longer trusted her. The king would hear about it. Her tears threatened her again and she cursed the day she'd ever laid eyes on the beautiful princess.

By nightfall her fear had hardened. She would take control of the city. It was the only option she had. The people needed to fear their queen as much as they loved and respected their absent king. She'd already sent her most loyal soldiers – some of whom were no doubt more than a little in love with her – to track down any messages that might have been sent from the castle. The king would not hear about this yet. He would not at all, if she could help it. She hadn't been through all of this to stumble now.

She went to her small room at the back of the library and locked the door. She placed several pieces of her gold jewellery into a small cast iron pot; trinkets and gifts from visiting ambassadors. From one of the cabinets she took a small vial and tipped some of the dust on top. Within seconds the gold began to melt and bubble. She smiled. She sipped her wine, enjoying the moment, and then carefully took the battered lamp from its place. She had a score to settle.

'Good try, Aladdin,' she whispered, leaning so close her face almost touched the surface and she could smell the tang of a thousand sweaty palms. 'Good try.'

She picked up a paintbrush and carefully painted the liquid gold across the surface of the lamp, covering every centimetre. No one would ever rub the magic bronze again. When she was finished she took what was left of the melted gold and poured it over the spout. Just in case. It cooled instantly, sealing the dangerous little boy in forever.

The queen was sure she could hear the tiniest echo of his frustrated scream.

It made her feel better.

4

'I want her heart'

It was a warm day in the forest and even though it made the hair on his chest tickle with sweat as he moved through the trees, that pleased the huntsman. Heat slowed animals as much as men and although his skills were such he'd had no doubt meat would roast over the fire tonight, the task was going to be easier than he'd expected. He could counter the laziness that came with the sun and force himself to be alert. It was unlikely to be the same for the animals in this dense woodland. So far, apart from an old crone scurrying between the trees just before he'd spied the stag, he'd seen little sign of human habitation and he'd heard no horn blowing for a royal hunt. It was wild here. He liked that.

These woods were new to him, but he tracked the white

beast easily enough, moving silently perhaps twenty feet or so behind it, his eyes scanning for the simplest of landmarks and storing them to memory. Following the animal would not be the problem. In his homeland the men born to the hunt could track even the lightest footed doe by the time they were ten. It was a matter of pride. Finding the kill was easy. Finding your way home afterwards could be harder. He'd spent one night lost in the forest when he was six and although that was now twenty years ago it was an experience that would stay with him until his dying day. He shook away the memory of those long hours of darkness and the unnatural wolf – a beast that still haunted his dreams – and moved steadily forward, sunlight cutting jagged hot paths through the heavy laden branches. The air was sweet with the fresh scent of unfamiliar greenery; citrus and leathery and sweet. He had no idea which of the kingdoms he was now in, whether they were friend or foe, but he was far from home, that was for certain.

His bag sat awkwardly on his back alongside his bow and arrows, and perhaps he should have left it at the campsite, but he'd learned a long time ago to keep the rewards of your hunts close. Man was the wiliest of creatures and very few could be trusted. Huntsmen grew up fast and he'd earned what he carried. The shoes he'd taken as a prize would stay with him.

The ground flattened for a while as the beast led him

near a rough edged track, beaten out by years of pounding hooves finding their way through the forest until it had become a lane of its own, but it didn't linger there long and turned back to its relative safety amidst the greenery.

The huntsman didn't hurry, instead allowing the creature to take in the beauty of this day in ignorance that there would be no more. Finally the trees thinned and opened out into a natural clearing with a narrow stream running through it.

Ahead the white stag, a rare beast, fine and noble, paused to drink. The huntsman dropped silently to the ground, stretching his body long against the earth. He pulled his bow free. His brown eyes narrowed as they studied the creature, small lines wrinkling his forehead and joining those that had sprung there early, the result of a life spent outdoors that was leaving him tanned and rugged before thirty. His heart beat fast against the ground and for a moment, as was always the case in these seconds before the kill, he felt everything in nature connect as one; him, the forest, the earth, and the stag itself. He watched as its thick neck lowered, its antlers dipping into the cool water, before it raised its head and shook the drops all over its glorious hide.

Without taking his eyes from the creature he shifted position, one arm tugging back the arrow until it was fighting him to spring free. White stags were rare and magical and notoriously difficult to track. They were protected from hunting, and belonged – if they could belong at all to anyone

– to the royal houses of the kingdoms. It was treason to take something which belonged to your king. Even with this thought, the huntsman's hand didn't waver. He was a stranger in this land. He had his own prince to honour. But more than that, he did not believe that any one life was more precious than another. Each creature that breathed was unique, so each death was equal. He respected them all.

He silently wished the animal safe passage. He wished it happiness in its moment of death. He closed his eyes and let the arrow fly true.

The stag fell without a sound. Its legs twitched momentarily and then it was still. The huntsman got to his feet, pleased with his work. It had been a clean kill and the animal had been unaware that death was coming. They should all have such a death.

He was so intent on skinning the stag, with the hunt now over and his senses no longer alert, that by the time he heard the soldiers crashing through the forest it was too late. He was surrounded.

'Put your knife down!'

The huntsman weighed up his options and it was clear he only had the one. He put the knife, thick with the animal's hot blood, on the ground next to the carcass. The black stallions, whose colour matched the black tabards and helmets of the men who rode them, pawed at the earth, excited by the proximity of death. It was an unnatural reaction, the huntsman thought. Horses, noble and beautiful as they might be, were natural prey, just like the stag. The blood should make them nervous.

'To kill a white stag is treason, you thieving bastard,' the captain said. 'The queen will want to deal with you herself!'

'The queen?' the huntsman asked. The tabards they wore were marked in blood red with a lion and serpent bound together. Was the queen the serpent? And in what land did a queen ever wield power?

'Not from round here, then?' a second soldier, one with a rougher accent, growled. 'That won't save you. The queen takes her magic very seriously. White stags are guardians of magic. You killed yourself when you killed it, boy.' The circle of men drew closer.

'An animal is just an animal,' the huntsman said, standing tall, his shoulders wide and with his dark eyes burning. 'I don't hold with superstition.'

The blow to the side of his head came hard and he fell to his knees, reeling and dazed, black spots filling the corners of his eyes. The men around him laughed, and he forced himself back to his feet.

'Shall we finish him off?' one voice said.

'No, tie him up,' the captain's eyes were cold through the gaps in his heavy helmet. 'We'll drag him back and let the queen deal with him. We're the Queen's Guard, after all.'

Two men leapt down from their horses and the

huntsman's jaw clenched as rough rope burned his skin as they tugged it tight around his arms.

'And bring his things.'

'What about the stag?'

'You two. Take it up to Ender's Pit and throw it in. Even the dwarves won't be able to get it out of there.'

As the soldiers dragged him out of the clearing, tugging the rope this way and that to shake him off balance, the huntsman tried not to think of the beast that he had now killed for nothing. To take any life was a serious business, that was the first lesson of the hunters. A death before its time must have value, whether it be to provide food or safety or shelter. The stag's now pointless death left a stain on the huntsman's soul. He would have his revenge for that, one way or another. He kept his feet solidly on the ground despite the men's attempts to topple him, but when they reached the track and the horses picked up their pace no man could have stayed upright. He did not scream though, even as the ground tore at his clothes and skin. He would not give them that.

The world spun by in a kaleidoscope of trees and light and sandy stones until they reached the edge of the forest where finally the track widened and levelled into a well used thoroughfare. It was no kinder to his battered body and the huntsman fought to keep his face twisted away from the ground. As blue sky replaced the wooded canopy, the shape of the kingdom laid itself out around him, strangely vast and oppressive when seen from the ground. He bit down on the inside of his mouth and tried to focus on anything but the searing pain through his shoulders as they threatened to pop free of their sockets. The land was the hunter's friend and knowing its layout could help him. A huntsman never gave up and at least the agony of his body was proof that, for now at least, he was still very much alive.

In the distance to the right was the Far Mountain which sat on the skyline of all the kingdoms, but here it was fringed with a range of jagged hills punctuated with dark patches from which black smoke rose in clouds. Mines, they had to be. And mines meant a dwarf land. He had never seen a dwarf although the tales of their small stature, long lives and hardy spirits had reached his own kingdom. To be so small forever was a strange concept to the hunter. How different the world must look.

A small rock was kicked up by a horse's hoof and caught his cheek, slicing it open slightly. He gasped and fought the urge to cry out. He would not give them the satisfaction of showing his weakness. Pain, like all things, his father had told him, passes. The few people who had come to the road from the patchy villages they passed, took a cursory glance at him and then scurried away. He caught a flash of pity on a few faces he was dragged by, but their glances all remained downcast and none came too close.

The Queen's Guard finally came to a halt outside the castle

walls, and as the huntsman rolled carefully onto his back and panted out his exhaustion he saw that different soldiers guarded the gates. These were dressed in a rich blue decorated with a gold lion on their chests. He recognised this uniform – and it wasn't of his own kingdom's alliance. They wore silver helmets that, unlike the Queen's Guard, did not cover their faces. Why were the Queen's Guard hiding their identities, he wondered. Were they unpopular or did the anonymity guarantee them more fear from the populace? Both were likely, judging by the bristling of both sets of soldiers' horses, reflecting the tension between the men who rode them.

The soldiers were certainly eyeing the Queen's Guard with a healthy dislike. The huntsman lay back and breathed hard into the dirt, happy just to have a moment of respite after being dragged so far.

Shadows fell across him and he looked up to see one of the soldiers in blue – an old dog with battle scars cutting across his weather beaten face – standing over him. He reached down and, with one strong tug, pulled the huntsman to his feet. The world spun madly for a moment as the agony in his arms became almost sweet in its exquisiteness, but as it faded to an excruciating throb he was pleased that, although he was swaying, his trembling legs hadn't failed him. It wasn't just dwarves who were hardy. The men of the hunt were born tough too and he would not let them down while so far from the forests of home.

'He killed a white stag. He deserved the ground,' the captain snarled. 'He's the queen's prisoner. One of ours. You have no right to touch him.'

'He may well be a traitor, and if so, then I'm sure he'll pay the price.' The second soldier remained where he was at the huntsman's side, defying any of the soldiers in black to knock the prisoner back down again. 'But our king, the Commander of *all* the guards, queen's and otherwise, respects bravery in all. This man hasn't screamed on the road. Not once. We'd have heard him.' He turned his head and spat into the dusty ground. 'We normally do. The king would allow him to face his fate on his feet.'

'The king isn't here, or haven't you noticed?'

'But he will be back. And I still outrank you, little brother.'

'So you do, Jeremiah, so you do.'

The huntsman looked from one to the other. Even though the captain's face was mostly covered by the lines of his helmet, he could see the two men had the same eyes. The same chin.

Although the captain still looked defiant, the huntsman knew he would stay on his feet for the rest of the journey. As the gates opened and they left the king's guard behind, he nodded slightly to Jeremiah. The soldier didn't respond and the huntsman hadn't expected him to, but thanks had still been required. He now owed the man a debt, just as he owed the white stag a life.

The city was full of life and energy, as were all the kingdoms this close to their castles. Merchants hurried this way and that with carts laden with cloths and fruit, from side streets came the clang of metal as blacksmiths worked on the ore from the mines and children ran between adults, ignoring the shouted reprimands and laughing as they chased each other. It seemed the city of his kingdom's enemy was not so very different in spirit to the city of his own. No wonder his father always shook his head and laughed quietly when they heard new stories of war. Their kings might have their battles, but a huntsman could talk to a huntsman and a baker could talk to a baker happily enough no matter what flag they served under.

He walked wearily forward as the small entourage took the centre of the road, no matter if there was someone already in their path or not. As quickly as the pedestrians cleared out of their way, so laughter died as they passed. One man spat in his face as he walked by, the warm thick liquid, rancid with tobacco, stinging the cut on his cheek, even though the man couldn't know what crime, if any, the huntsman was being dragged in for. As he stepped back the man looked to the guards for approval and then glanced upwards. A small twitch at the corner of his mouth betrayed his fear.

The ravens perched so still on the rooftops were out of place against the brightness of the wealthy city, filled as it was with ornate buildings and shiny clear glass windows.

This kingdom was winning its skirmishes and it had the mines, and therefore plenty of strong metal which so many of the kingdoms lacked. No doubt much of the metal scraped from the heart of the earth made its way to his own alliance. Traders didn't let wars get in the way of business and kings didn't let wars get in the way of revenue. There was affluence here. The market squares were lined with pale sandstone and the closer they drew to the white castle at the core of the city, the richer the stones became, glinting with shards of crystal in the sunshine.

He let his hair fall across his face to shade his eyes as he studied the ravens above them. There were too many of them, perched every twenty yards or so on a turret or chimney. They made no noise and their eyes, shining like the tiniest black pearls from the Meridian Sea, darted this way and that. They were watching the activity on the streets below. One met the huntsman's gaze as he walked beneath it and the bird stared back, coldly fixated. Despite the events of the past months the huntsman still didn't really understand the politics of cities and princes, but he did know wildlife. This behaviour wasn't natural. He had no fear of ravens – they had done nothing to deserve their reputation as a bad omen. It was just a bird of a differing feather to a dove. This bird's feathers though, were decidedly unruffled.

The huntsman dropped his gaze, having seen all he needed. The ravens were enchanted. He was sure of it.

* * *

It felt like they marched up hundreds of stairs before they reached the highest tower of the castle, where the queen was waiting. The huntsman had lost count by the time they got to the top, but as the soldiers' boots echoed on the black marble floor all the huntsman could see through the arched windows was the sky. A cool breeze, much sharper than the warm wind below, caught him and he shivered. Were they so high they were almost among the clouds? And why would the queen of such a rich land have her throne room so far above her people?

Finally they reached a vast circular room high in the tower. The walls here were as black as the stone beneath their feet, but the solid colour was broken up by patterns and streaks of crimson red, the decoration sharp and jagged like winter branches that had stretched up through the floor, far from wherever their roots might be in the castle below. It looked like unnatural veins on black skin to the huntsman.

In the centre of the room was a solitary throne made of cast black ore and lined with luxurious red velvet cushioning. The huntsman took in a deep breath. Everything here was new. Opulent and impressive as it all was, these had not been the queen's rooms for long. There were no scents in the crisp and brittle air as if even the summer outside didn't dare venture in.

At the back, an ornate archway led to a smaller room and as the guards threw him to the floor and he slid forward a few feet, he caught a glimpse of strange objects laid on soft cushions and locked in sparkling glass cases. A shadow fell across his line of sight and behind him the guards stood to attention. The queen had arrived.

Her footsteps were delicate and her stride short as her heeled feet tapped over to stop before him. The huntsman's dark eyes rose from the cold floor and for a moment his aches and pains were forgotten. She was beautiful. Her hair was like the ice on the sheer walls of the Far Mountain. Her lips were pink hearts from the highest branches of the blossom tree and her eyes were so blue and cold they stung him to look into them. He'd seen winter wolves who looked like that just as spring began to ease the rest of nature's suffering but start their own. Pure defiance, even though they knew their time to chase the frost to a different kingdom or die had likely come. Winter wolves, so much smaller and more ethereal than their grey rough brothers, were beautiful, delicate and dangerous. This queen was no different.

'I see you're still taking orders from your big brother,' she said, her eyes on the captain.

'I had to, your Majesty. He's the senior ranking officer. What else could I do?'

'You'd do well to remember that the king will not be returning home soon. I'm told his campaign is doing well and he's pushing towards the sea. He says he might not be back for another two years.' The soldier shuffled awkwardly under the intensity of her icy gaze.

'That's a long time. Terrible things can happen to people – or their families – in that time. The dwarves always need ore sorters, and sadly, as we all know, only dwarves' lungs can cope with the dust for very long. If you feel uncomfortable serving in my guard then I'm sure I can find a use for you elsewhere, Captain Cricket. And remember, in his absence, I am the voice of the king himself.'

'It won't happen again, your Majesty.' The captain quickly tugged open the huntsman's rough hemp bag. 'The prisoner had these on him. I thought you might want them.'

The diamond slippers. Of course. The huntsman watched as the queen's irritation with her servant vanished at the sight of the sparkling shoes. As the light hit them and refracted, all the colours in the rainbow dazzled in their surfaces. The queen's beautiful eyes widened and her mouth opened slightly. He knew why. The slippers were warm to the touch. They tingled with charm and charisma. He'd felt it when he'd taken them from that very different kingdom, and he'd heard their story since. There was more than precious stones in their making.

'Slippers for a ball,' the queen whispered. 'And with such magic in them.' She looked down at the huntsman again, this time with far more curiosity. 'And he killed a white stag?'

'In the heart of the forest. I ordered my men to throw it into Ender's Pit.'

'Not a fitting burial for such a beast. But at least no peasant will eat it.'

The huntsman could smell the relief in the sharp tang of the captain's sweat, but it was overwhelmed by the warmth radiating from the queen's skin. How could someone so cold on the surface have so much heat inside her? His own heart beat faster. He was a huntsman, after all, and proximity to danger always excited him. How old was she, this queen? Younger than him, for sure. He met her gaze.

'You can leave us,' she said, still not looking up at her men. They didn't protest, and the huntsman wondered what kind of weapons this delicate beauty had in her arsenal that made her men sure they could leave her with a killer and she'd be safe. Magic, it had to be. He'd learned a lot about magic in the past few weeks – it was more powerful than any blade. Not that he had a blade. Even if he did, he'd find it hard to use on this exquisite creature.

As the soldiers left he got to his feet, regardless of a lack of permission. The queen didn't comment, merely studied him as he rose. He stood several inches taller than her but she didn't step back. She was not afraid of him, that was for sure.

'Where did you get these?' She held up the slippers and the sunshine they reflected danced across her flawless face.

'I earned them.' It was the truth in a way. She was watching him thoughtfully and he examined her in turn. She was even younger than he'd thought, a second wife to the king perhaps. How did she like that? Was it the cause of the hardness in her eyes

'The words of many a thief. They have magic in them. Did you know that?'

'I don't hold with magic.'

'I can see that. If you did you wouldn't have killed my stag.'

'It was the forest's stag, not yours,' the huntsman said. 'We're all just beasts. We all breathe. No one creature is more valuable than another.' He paused, the memory of the stag still fresh. 'And no death must be wasted.'

'All life is equal,' she finished, stealing his unspoken words from him. 'All death is equal.' She smiled at his surprise, her white teeth small and perfect. 'We had tribes of huntsmen like you in my homeland. Men who lived by the code.' She took a step closer to him and his heart beat faster. Could she sense his rising excitement? What game was she playing with him?

'What about your own life?' she asked, looking up at him and standing so near that he could feel her warm breath on his skin. 'Are you so casual about that?'

'That one,' he smiled, 'I have to say, I am more careful with than others'.'

'That tends to be the case.' She held up the slippers. 'I shall keep these for now.'

'The words of many a thief.' The atmosphere between them was charged and the huntsman's blood rushed hot through his body. The ache in his muscles was almost forgotten.

'You should watch your mouth.'

'If I'm going to die I'm not sure what difference my words could make.'

'I was going to offer you a deal.' This time she did take a step back and he saw the slightest shift in her posture as her spine stiffened. She was the queen again. What was she hiding? Why were there so many layers of defences around the queen in the clouds?

'What kind of deal?'

'The kind where you do as you're told and you get to keep your life.' Her mouth twisted; tight with bitterness. 'But it does involve taking another one. Something you seem to be adept at.'

'But you have a whole guard for that.'

'There are some lengths,' she turned away from him and moved towards the window, 'that I wouldn't ask my men to go to. For some tasks, you need an outsider. I also want it done cleanly and with respect.' She didn't look at him as she spoke, her voice dropping until he had to strain to hear her.

'She hasn't been in the castle much. Not for a while. Not since I banished the dwarves from the inner city and replaced her maids with some of my own. Now she comes in late at night and goes out in the early morning. I hear whispers about her, though. Helping the poor, riding through the streets and distributing her father's alms. The kindest, the most gracious, fairest princess in all the kingdoms. That's what they say. They're running out of superlatives.'

The huntsman wondered how much she was talking to him and how much to herself. She was lost in her own thoughts, and as the light caught her face for a moment he thought he saw another animal beneath her cool surface. A rare creature, one who had been hidden so long that perhaps she'd forgotten that she even existed. He felt himself stir despite his torn muscles and aching body.

'She'll be in the forest somewhere. I hear that's where she spends her days.'

'You seem to hear a lot for someone who prefers the top of a tower to having the warm grass beneath her feet.' He moved closer until he was standing only a foot or so behind her.

'I have eyes everywhere,' she said. He thought of the ravens sitting so still on the rooftops. Ethereally beautiful she might be, but she was damaged and dangerous. He wanted her, he couldn't deny that, but this would be no conquest. There would be no love in it. Not from her.

'How will I recognise her?' he asked.

'Oh, there is no one quite like Snow White. You'll know when you've found her.' She turned to face him. 'But just in case...' She tilted her head back, her neck as slim and pale and strong as the swans' on the great lake, and opened up a locket at her throat. He leaned closer, to both look and also to feel her heat again. He had been on the road a long time and there had been plenty of danger and little earthly pleasure. He tore his eyes away from her pale skin and looked at the pictures. On one side was the image of a middle-aged man; thick set and piggy eyed. If this image was a flattering likeness then the huntsman was not surprised the queen was so unhappy. The other frame held the image of a full-lipped dark haired beauty whose eyes, even trapped by an artist's pen, danced with merriment and joy at life.

'I want her heart,' the queen said softly, before snapping the locket shut. 'You will bring it to me or I will cut yours out myself.' From within the folds of her delicate gown, she pulled out a hunting knife. 'Finest dwarf silver and steel. It will make it quick. And don't even think about running. The forest is deep but my guards will find you.'

She didn't hand him the knife but instead stepped closer, tugged at his belt and holstered it there. He looked down at the swell of her breasts trapped tightly in the bones of her dress. He was hardening and her hands were so close he wondered if she was aware of it.

He was still covered in dirt and sweat and both the stag's dried blood and his own, and her fingers drifted across the stains on his clothes as if fascinated by them. Finally she looked up at him and he could see in the endless lakes of her eyes, where good and bad and everything in between darted like fish in their icy depths, that she knew exactly what effect she was having on him.

'Why are you so sad?' he asked.

She pulled back slightly, shocked. 'Why would you say that?'

He moved fast, reaching in and taking her face in his hands. His mouth was on hers, soft and sweet and so far from the taste of the forest, before she could stop him. His tongue pushed against her protesting one for a long moment and then she broke free. She stared at him, panting slightly, and for the first time she looked like a young woman rather than a queen.

'I can taste it on you,' he said.

'Bullshit.'

'Not exactly royal language.' He laughed aloud, unable to stop himself. 'Dragged up in the streets, were you, before the king found you?'

'You know nothing about me,' she spat at him. 'Nothing.'

'Except that you are filled with sadness.' He grabbed her arms and she struggled against him, but he held her firmly as he pulled her close. She wasn't really fighting him, he knew that. She was fighting herself. She had magic. If she wanted to stop him, she could no doubt kill him where he stood. He'd be helpless against her. That excited him further. Danger had always been his Achilles' heel. He leaned forward to kiss her again.

'You revolt me,' she said.

'You prefer your fat, old king?' he whispered. He kissed her again, tenderly this time, and the tension eased in her arms. Her hard shell was cracking. Her hot mouth tasted of fresh orchard apples. This was not love, he knew, not even a hint of it in the meeting of their lips, but it was a release they both needed. His body ached. He was tired. And he wasn't out of the woods yet. This woman, this strange queen would strike him dead if she wanted to.

He broke away to breathe, blood pumping loud in his ears. She was not trustworthy, but she was beautiful and sensuous and aloof. She was different to him in many ways, that was true, but they were both predators. He watched her for a moment, her head tilted slightly backwards, her pale breasts rising and falling fast within the constraints of her dress. Her eyes were shut, and he was surprised to see a tear squeeze out and run like a winter stream down her pale face. He wiped it away with his rough fingers.

'Just make her go away,' the queen whispered, as his hands reached for her corset laces and freed her hot skin. 'Just make her go away. I have no choice anymore.' With her eyes firmly shut, she kissed him back and pulled him to the ground. For a while, the stag and his past adventures, and the killing to come, were entirely forgotten.

It didn't take him long to track Snow White. People were creatures of habit and her horse's hooves had scored their mark in the paths leading into the thickest part of the forest at the base of the mountain. Even without them to guide him he'd have searched that way. The dwarves were her friends and the dwarves lived at the base of the mountain within whose guts they toiled for such long hours. She came this way each morning and left each night to head back to the castle. Animal tracks never lied.

The sun was hot as it cut through the canopy and he glanced up occasionally to scour the branches for ravens, but he hadn't seen a single one since he'd left the city walls behind, hidden on the back of a merchant's cart. Perhaps the queen's control over the birds had a physical limit. Still, he didn't relax. There would be soldiers behind him before long and there was no doubt she'd have doubled the patrols on the borders of the kingdom. Whatever moment they'd shared – and she'd been so cold about it when they were done that he'd almost thought it was a dream – no trust had come with it.

There had been no affection in what they'd done. The

strange beauty had kept her eyes closed from start to finish, murmuring words he couldn't quite make out as he explored her body and took his satisfaction from it. It was the huntsman's way until true love found them, but this time he was the one who came away feeling awkward afterwards. They had used each other – there was no denying that – but he knew that she had used him more. If she'd had any respect for him beforehand, there was none in evidence when she finally sent him on his way. Maybe he had been foolish, but there had been too much wickedness around him of late and nothing shook that away like the pleasures of the body, whether they be taken with a queen or a serving girl.

He concentrated on the task she'd set him. He was a straightforward man, but he was learning the wiles of the wealthy. It seemed that no matter how much he wished for a quiet life, fate had drawn him into royal games once again, and this one would have a twist in it before it was done. There was still a debt that needed paying and he wouldn't forget it.

Ahead, just out of sight, a horse whinnied and pawed at the leafy ground. His skin prickled and he edged silently forward, ignoring the tiny insects which hovered and darted around his head in the muggy heat. The air so close to the base of the mountain carried a tang of minerals from the mines, and as he peered through the low branches to the pool beyond, it grew stronger. A thick mist coated the surface of the water, thinning into steam as if the water was warmer than the air. Perhaps it was. There were no mines in his homeland and who knew how the metals in the earth changed its nature.

From somewhere in the haze came splashing, light and free, and as he was sure that he couldn't see her then he believed the reverse must also be true; he slipped between the trees until he was in the clearing beside a fine horse with royal colours in its reins. He patted the thick black neck and calmed it, impressed by its size and strength; not the steed he expected for a princess. Dark eyes full of fire watched him warily. This was no prancing pony, this was a stallion fit for a fighting king. What was it about the women in this royal family that made them so strange? An ice queen in a tower and a princess with a knight's horse who swam – he took the pair of riding breeches and white shirt from the horse's back to find her underclothes there too – naked in the forest? There was nothing normal about this – but then, with his adventures of late, normality was becoming a rarity. He hid behind the thickest willow trunk and waited.

She emerged from the water not long after, standing on the bank and tipping her head back to squeeze the water from her black hair, as naked as the day of her birth and brazenly comfortable with it. Suddenly, he understood the horse. Where the queen chose to hide in her tower, this princess was earthy, a creature of nature. Her slim legs were long and firm and she moved with the grace of the finest white stag. This was no delicate animal; no skittish forest deer. She was beautiful without a doubt, but not fragile. She was fuller figured and rounder featured than her step-mother – generosity made flesh. Her stride was confident and sunlight glittered on the drops of water that clung to her skin like jewels. She paused and stretched, smiling at the mix of warm air and cool liquid on her drying body.

That was what was so wrong with the queen, he realised as he watched the girl so comfortable in her nudity. She was equally beautiful but with none of the freedom or calm of this princess she hated. She was harder. One day she'd harden so much the pressure would shatter her.

Snow White paused and frowned, and before she had time to realise she wasn't alone, the huntsman stepped out in front of her. He held up her clothes.

'Looking for these?'

She crouched slightly, making ready to fight, but made no effort to cover her glorious nakedness and her eyes darted here and there searching for a potential weapon. He liked her more already.

'I'm not here to harm you,' he said. 'Well, technically I'm here to kill you, but she owes me a life in exchange for one she wasted, and so I choose to spare yours.' This girl's life for the stag's would be a good payment. One creature of nature for another. He held out her clothes but instead of reaching for them, she'd been distracted by something else. Her eyes widened as she spotted the elegant knife tucked into his belt.

'That's a royal blade,' she said. Her voice was as rich and sweet as her curves. 'Where did you get it, thief? And if you're looking for riches,' she raised her arms and one eyebrow, 'as you can see, I'm not hiding any.'

'That's the second time a beautiful woman has called me a thief today and neither time has it been true.'

'I don't believe you.' She snatched her shirt and glared at him while tugging it over her still damp skin. He could see from the saddle that she rode like a man, the horse firmly clamped between her thighs, and his eyes fell to examining the taut muscles. He wondered how it would feel to be gripped by them. 'There's only one person who could have given you that knife and that's my...' She fell silent as the truth dawned on her. '...my step-mother.' She stood and stared at him for a moment as if willing him to deny it, but he said nothing. Eventually, she came towards him and searched his face. '*She* sent you? To kill me?' She looked down at the knife again. 'But why? Why would she...? I thought... it was all a misunderstanding so why would she...?' Tears welled up in her eyes. 'She hates me,' she whispered. 'She really hates me.'

'You can't go back to the castle,' the huntsman said. Heat rose under his collar. Women's tears were something he didn't understand. In fact women, beyond their physical aspects, were something he didn't understand, and nothing he'd seen in the past few weeks had done anything to change that. 'Go somewhere you can hide for a while. Until your father returns from his campaigns. Do you have people you can trust?'

'It was all a lie. Everything she said. She *was* trying to kill me. Why would she want to kill me?' She was lost in her own thoughts, and he dropped the rest of her clothes in order to grab her arms and shake her slightly. There was no time for this. Her skin was warm and supple.

'Listen to me! Do you have people you can trust?'

It took a moment for her to focus, but finally she nodded. Her tears were still falling and she sniffed hard. 'Yes. Yes, I do.'

'Good,' he said. 'I'll take a deer's heart back instead.'

'She wants my heart?' She laughed and then choked on the fresh tears. 'My *heart?*'

'I'll have to take your horse,' the huntsman said. 'It will make it more believable. She doesn't trust me.' This brought a fresh wave of tears and he wondered if she was listening to him at all, but she patted the horse's neck and then pressed her face into it. Finally, she looked up at him. 'Thank you,' she said.

'She owed me a life,' he answered, simply. The queen, who claimed to know the huntsman's code, had not realised how closely he lived by it. Regardless of the danger it might place him in, the stag's wasted life demanded the balance was restored. The weeping princess threw her arms around his neck and hugged him tight, a sudden gesture he had no time to pull back from. Her body was warm through his clothes, her nipples pressing into him through his thin shirt. His arms folded around her, his hands on the taut curve of her back, fighting the urge to slip them down to the rise of her buttocks.

'Thank you,' she repeated. After a moment, she stiffened in his arms. 'I can smell her on you,' she said, pulling back slightly before pushing her face into his neck and breathing deeply. She looked up at him. 'It's her. You've *been* with her.' Between her body pressed against his and her breath on his skin, the huntsman couldn't stop himself responding. She could feel it, he was sure. What was going on today?

'If you tell your father,' he said, roughly, 'it won't just be her head he takes. It will be mine too. He tried to step back, but she kept her arms around him. They were strong and he could feel the lean muscles beneath her skin.

'What did you do with her?' she asked, her eyes drifting half shut, tears still falling. 'Touch me like you touched her. Touch me like she touched you.' The huntsman said nothing, once again feeling like a pawn in a game he hadn't signed up to play. Soldiers would be coming to find him if he didn't return soon. And this girl was a princess, not a wicked queen. She should not be touched by any man before her wedding day. Not even by the man saving her life. He felt the strands of the web he was trapped in tightening around him as she pressed her body into his and lifted her lips. 'Kiss me like she kissed you,' she whispered, all hot breath and warm skin. 'Please.'

And, cursing his own nature, he did.

5

'A curse is always the thing, you know'

The first thing the queen did was take her knife from him. The blade was still bloody and sticky to the touch. For a moment she felt faint and swayed on her feet. Flashes of imagined scenes hit her in a wave; Snow White bleeding to death in the forest, her eyes widening as the metal cut into her chest, the huntsman's hand pulling her warm, dead flesh apart to find the trophy that would secure his own freedom.

She stared at the weapon. What had she done? The stark reality of it was like ice in her veins and she tightened her grip on the hilt to stop her hand trembling so obviously. 'Did she suffer?'

'No,' the huntsman answered levelly. He looked so calm. Was he as much of a monster as she? She drew herself up tall and haughty; playing the part that was becoming her. What was done was done and there was no magic that could undo it. She really was the wicked queen now. It was time to live up to that.

'Where did you put her body?' She took the filthy knife and resheathed it, not wanting to look too long on the blood that coated it.

'Ender's Pit,' he said and then handed her the pouch. It was heavier than she'd expected. A butcher's wrap of meat like those she'd carried for her mother when she was small. Blood seeped out through the roughly sewn edges. She didn't open it. She didn't want to see.

'And now if I can have my slippers I'll be on my way. A deal's a deal and I have unfinished business elsewhere.' He didn't let his eyes, deep and unfathomable, drop from hers. He was rough and handsome and arrogant, this travelling stranger, and she detested him. She wanted to sink the knife into his neck and be done with the whole damned business.

'Of course.' Around them, the walls blackened further and the red jagged lines sprouted new crimson branches. This room was her forest of magic and as her heart hardened, her power grew stronger. Her lips tightened into a smile that was as sharp as the murderous blade. It was for the best. All of it was.

'Are these what he wants, dear?' The familiar voice cracked like dry forest twigs under children's running feet.

'They're very pretty. In fact, I'm very impressed with your entire collection. You've done well.'

Lilith didn't look round as the old woman shuffled out from the back room. Her great-grandmother had arrived unannounced only an hour earlier and she hadn't had time to process it yet. The day had been surreal enough without her. As far as Lilith knew or remembered the old woman had never left her candy cottage, and yet here she was. She had trekked across kingdoms and turned up as if she'd been just passing. She was also doing that hunched over, helpless little old lady thing that she slipped into whenever she had an agenda. The huntsman's face crinkled in disgust at the sight of her and Lilith felt a surge of pride in her bloodline. Women put too much store in beauty as a power to wield over men. There were other powers which were just as valuable. She was learning that.

'Yes. They're his. He can have them back.'

'No need to be hasty.' The crone placed the shoes on the floor beside the wide cushioned throne, out of reach of the huntsman. 'You were always in such a hurry. Even as a child.' She took the pouch from Lilith's hands and her gnarled hands pulled on the drawstrings.

'You don't need to look in there.' Her heart raced slightly and she flushed, just as she'd done as a child when she'd been caught peeling a strip of liquorice from the walls, black juice smeared around her mouth. There was no need for her great-grandmother to know what she'd done. She didn't want anyone to know what she'd done.

'Oh, you should always check the goods before you pay, my dear.' She tipped the heart into her hand. Glistening meat. The queen felt sick.

'Oh my,' the old woman said, turning it over in her hands until they were covered in redness. 'I see.' She slid it back into the sopping cloth and then licked her fingers, savouring the taste. Her lips smacked together and her eyes twinkled. 'But those shoes? For a deer's heart? It's not much of a trade.'

'What? It's not...?' Lilith stared at her and then at the huntsman, whose eyes darted from the pouch to the old woman and then to the queen again.

'Did you think it was a human heart?'

'I...' Heat burned her from the inside. 'But...'

'I know the taste, dear,' the old woman said, 'and this is not to my taste.' She tutted at the huntsman. 'I fear you've been a little deceptive, young man.'

'Where is she?' Blood rushed to the queen's face and she seized the knife and stepped forward, jabbing it towards him. 'You let her go?' A whirl of emotions gripped her and for the first time she saw fear in the huntsman's face. She liked it. 'Was it her beauty? Is that what stopped you? Was her beauty worth your own precious life?' He stepped backwards slightly and her angry glare darted at the vast doors beyond which slammed immediately shut.

'Very nice, Lilith dear,' her great-grandmother said, approvingly.

'You wouldn't understand,' he said.

'Why?' The dark snakes in her soul writhed. 'Because I don't have her charm? Her beauty? Because I'm filled with poison?' Her words were the dry hiss of a trapped animal. Fear was eating at her anger. If Snow White was still alive then where was she? Already sending messages to her father? Was the executioner's block all her own future now held? The people wouldn't mourn their cold, unfriendly queen. Would the king call her a witch for real and burn her? Were the flames that haunted her finally going to claim her?

'Did she give herself to you to set her free?'

A nerve twitched in his cheek as the arrow of truth in her words struck home. Her anger burned brighter, a white heat that could turn a city to dust.

'You think you're such a righteous man,' she sneered, not caring that it made her ugly. 'You're not. You're nothing but a mouse.' She spat the last word out and a jolt of energy shot through her arm.

The huntsman vanished.

For a moment she couldn't understand what had happened, and then, as her great-grandmother cackled and clapped applause, she heard the tiniest of squeaks. A small brown field mouse was scurrying across the floor.

'Much better!' the crone said. 'A mouse. Very good. A

fitting punishment for a double crossing huntsman. Let's see how he survives the forest now.' She snapped her fingers and the mouse was gone. Lilith stared at the empty patch of floor and then looked over at her great-grandmother. The old woman was smiling.

'Don't worry, dear. He'll be back one day.' She patted the throne. 'Have a sit down.' Lilith did as she was told and the old woman looked into the pouch once again. 'Cutting out a heart. I do sympathise with the sentiment, but death is so...' she paused. 'Final. No magic can change it.'

Lilith looked at her great-grandmother and thought of all the small bones that littered her garden. 'And you should know.'

'I only want what's best for you, dear. Don't be irritable. It doesn't suit you.'

'What am I going to do?' She just wanted to cry.

'A curse is always the thing, you know.' Her great-grandmother nudged her along the seat and squeezed her bony hips into the throne to share it. 'Death is a last resort. Curses, well, they give you power.'

'Then I'd like to curse her to sleep forever,' Lilith said. She was aware that her voice had taken on the slightly surly tone of her youth.

'Forever is a long time,' her great-grandmother said. 'Aside from death, the only thing that lasts for ever is true love.' She rummaged in the folds of her raggedy clothes and pulled out a rosy apple. 'Eat this. They're good for you.'

Lilith took it and bit in, chewing the crisp, sweet flesh, hoping it could cleanse the bitter remnants of hate that filled her mouth. 'Then I want her to sleep until true love's kiss wakes her.'

'Now you're getting the hang of it.' The old lady nodded approvingly. 'That one's always a winner.'

Lilith leaned her head on the bony shoulder beside her. It was good to be with someone who loved her.

'Leave it with me.' Her great-grandmother patted her leg affectionately. 'I'll take care of it on my way home. It'll all work out in the end. I'm like your fairy godmother, eh?'

Lilith shut her eyes and let the old woman soothe her. 'It's good to see you, Granny,' she said, quietly. 'It really is.'

6

'No good can come from a crone'

They didn't speak much as they came down the mountain from the mine. Despite the hardiness that came from their nature and a lifetime of working underground, it still took a while to recover any energy after a full shift. Even as they reached the edge of the forest the three dwarves didn't sing as the hot metal in their lungs was cooled by the fresh open air. Their minds were occupied with the secret they shared and as soon as their feet marched in steady rhythm onto the soft grass, their eyes were darting this way and that for evidence of soldiers. They had a princess to protect. Dwarf honour was second to none – as was so often the way with people so long subjugated – and they had vowed to keep their friend safe. If they failed in their promise, a terrible fate would befall them. Dwarves never broke an oath.

It was a warm day, but the swarms of tiny flies that filled the damp air stayed clear of them as they made their way past the hot pool and towards the path home, hovering high above the short statured dwarves. The rest of the team would follow soon, but these three, whose real names hadn't been used in so long they'd almost forgotten what they were, had earned themselves an early finish. Grouchy took the lead, Dreamy behind him, and Stumpy, his nickname earned after he'd been pulled screaming from beneath a rock slide, his crushed hand missing, followed behind them. They were lost in their own thoughts for most of the journey until they reached the crossroads. Dreamy paused, his feet breaking their marching rhythm and his companions stopped beside him.

A figure was shuffling along the worn path. Even with her head bowed the glaring warts that covered her nose and chin were visible and her hair hung in grey strings. Her dress, a mixture of worn rags cobbled together into some kind of shroud-like garment had perhaps once been black but was long faded to grey. 'A crone,' Dreamy muttered, his eyes narrowing. 'No good can come from a crone.'

The old woman raised a hand in greeting and hobbled closer. She smiled and Dreamy shivered at the blackness in the gaps where so many missing teeth should have been. 'Travel safely, ma'am.' Grouchy nodded to her, tipping his hat as if he were a gentleman of the court rather than a dwarf with black mine dust so ingrained on his skin that he could no longer scrub it off.

'I thank you, young man.' The words were weak and came out in a hiss of air that whistled through her gums. She was carrying a basket and under the checked cloth, Dreamy could just make out a large, perfectly red and waxy apple. His mouth watered slightly. She started to hobble away from them and then paused, her wizened head creaking round on her brittle shoulders until she'd fixed them with one watery eye.

'I saw a thing,' she said, 'that might be useful to you. A deer. Dead a little way back in the shade of a great willow. Straight from here as the crow flies. Looked fresh.' She paused. 'You look hungry.'

'We have to get back to our cottage,' Dreamy said. His skin tingled warily even though she was an old woman and he was a hardy dwarf with thirty years mining under his belt and an axe hanging across his back.

'Fair enough. Something in the forest will have it. Fresh meat rarely goes to waste.' He raised a hand to say farewell, but she'd already turned and continued her slow shuffle along the path. The dwarves didn't move.

'A deer.' Stumpy licked his lips loudly. 'A fresh one.' Dreamy knew how he felt. His stomach had rumbled at the mention of the animal. Tonight, all seven dwarves would be home and most of what they'd eat would be boiled potatoes and cabbage, flavoured with a few herbs and the juice of a boiled scrawny rabbit carcass all the meat of which had been eaten days before. Now they also had Snow White to feed – a royal princess. The small forest animals who weakened at the mountain's edge were not good enough for her, no matter how she protested that their generosity in hiding her was banquet enough.

As Grouchy and Stumpy muttered between themselves, Dreamy watched the old woman slowly making her way along the path that they should have been taking home instead of lingering here. 'No good comes from a crone,' he repeated.

'You can't judge a book by its cover,' Grouchy snorted with mild amusement. 'She might just be an old grandmother visiting nearby.'

'What would you know about books?' Dreamy said. 'You've never even read one.'

Grouchy was their unofficial leader, his rank in the mine granting him the same authority in the cottage and it was rare for any of them to snap at him, least of all Dreamy, the gentlest of them all. But there was something about this crone that unsettled him.

Snow White had brought Dreamy books, slim volumes of adventures that she'd sneaked out of the vast library in the castle. They had changed Dreamy's world and he would always love her for that alone.

'Don't need to read one to see how they've addled your

brain,' Grouchy said. 'But then, your head's always been in the clouds.'

'The stories keep me sane while my body is in the mines,' Dreamy said. The old woman was almost out of sight now.

'Music should do that,' Stumpy said. 'Music is the dwarf way.' He spat on the ground. 'We should at least look for that deer. I'm fucking starving.'

Dreamy didn't argue. Two to one said they should try, and his own stomach was turning against him in the argument. Venison was a strong meat. A delicious meat. And a whole deer would last them a while.

They found the carcass barely ten minutes along the path the old woman had been following and she hadn't lied. It lay beneath a willow tree on cool ground. The meat was in good condition. More than that, with its heart cut out, it was clearly the deer the huntsman had killed to trick the queen. 'We have to take it,' Grouchy said. 'It's evidence that Snow White is still alive. We can't have the Queen's Guard finding it, and find it they will before long.' They roped its legs with vines and Dreamy used his axe to hack down a long branch from a tree which they could strap it to. When the dead animal was secured, Grouchy took one end and Dreamy the other, leaving Stumpy to carry their tools as best he could, and by the time they were back at the crossroads and heading home

Dreamy's misgivings about the crone had passed. She'd been a blessing as it turned out. They would all eat well and the princess's survival would stay secret. He smiled and even joined in as the other two began to hum a working tune.

Finally a thin, barely visible line of worn ground branched off from the main path and the dwarves turned on to it. Their cottage was only twenty feet or so away but was still completely invisible to the naked eye. Even if the crone had been of wicked intent she'd have walked right past it. He shook his head slightly and laughed at his own nervousness. No one ever found dwarf cottages, and theirs had become considerably better protected in the past twenty-four hours. The forest had a tendency to wrap itself around dwarf cottages. Bushes and trees were thicker and heavy roots broke the ground's surface ready to trip any passer-by who came too close. Branches hung so low that anyone taller than a young child would have to duck to find their way through, and Snow White aside – because every one, even the forest, could see the goodness in her – would then find themselves tangled in and stabbed at by errant twigs they hadn't noticed were there. Brambles would creep out and dig into skin until finally any curiosity would be overwhelmed and the interloper would back away, no longer interested in the hints of life they'd spotted through the bushes. It wasn't that the dwarves wanted to hide, it was just that they liked what little privacy they had, and nature respected that. Nature was a magic in itself. It took care of those who loved it.

As they passed under the last of the thick branches, the clearing opened up in front of them and their cottage, bathed in golden sunshine, came into view. Dreamy smiled. Grouchy had been right. He was too caught up in his world of stories. Snow White, dressed in her riding breeches and shirt, was sitting on the heavy wooden table where they all ate out side in the summer. A bowl of peeled potatoes was to her right and a tankard sat to her left. Dwarf ale, of course. She could drink the heady mix with the best of them and sing along until dawn when the occasion arose, her beautiful face shining with earthy joy. The thought stabbed at his insides.

He wished she could shake this terrible sadness that was on her. She'd refused to send a message to her father. She'd cried. A lot. They hadn't really known what to do about that. Dwarves didn't cry that much and as far as they'd known neither did Snow White. They'd brought her drink and forced her to eat something and left her to work it out of her system. That had been Dreamy's suggestion. There were lots of women in the stories he'd been reading and he'd learned that sometimes they just needed to be left alone to think. More of the stories would have turned out better if the men had seen that as clearly as Dreamy did.

At least today she was up and keeping busy. Maybe it would all work out all right. He grinned and waved and she gave them a soft smile in return before raising something to her mouth. Dreamy froze as he saw what it was. An apple; large and impossibly red and waxy. He tried to cry out – to stop her taking a bite – but the words choked in his throat.

No good can come of a crone.

Her eyes widened as she took the first crisp bite and as the dwarves dropped the deer and started to run, she was on her feet and clawing at her neck. Her legs buckled and, with the rest of the apple still gripped tightly in her hand, she fell lifeless to the forest floor.

With shattered hearts they searched the forest for the crone but there was no sign of her. She had vanished, leaving them no outlet for their anger. When the other four marched back to the cottage and discovered the awful events, the dwarves mourned, singing low songs into the moonlight and through until dawn. The deer began to rot where it had been dropped, a symbol of their stupidity that they taunted themselves with.

They pushed their small beds together and laid Snow White out across them, the apple still gripped in her cold fingers. They lit candles around her. They sang some more. They discovered that dwarves could cry. Over the next few days they worked long, dangerous shifts for extra gold and then Dreamy spent everything they had saved on a beautiful pink and white dress, bought from a passing merchant on his way to the fine ladies of the city.

In the clearing the deer stank and mouldered in the heat, but Snow White neither breathed nor rotted. Grouchy worked through the night forging a glass coffin, and on the third day they washed and gently redressed her, curling her long hair and rouging her lips and cheeks. When she was ready, they carried the coffin to the mound on the other side of the thicket where it was rare for any one but a dwarf to pass. Bluebells grew on the banks and the sun caught the space all year round. They would not put her underground. They knew better than any how harsh and brutal the earth's grip could be. She would lie in the sun, just as she had loved to do.

Some of the dwarves thought that perhaps she should have been dressed in the breeches she'd loved too but Dreamy was so distraught that they let him make a proper princess of her. She was a princess, after all. They would guard her until her father returned, and then perhaps one day a cure for the curse would be found.

They sat with her when their long, bone-tiring shifts were done, but it was always Dreamy who stayed with her the longest. Her sadness was over – his had begun.

Dreamy was sitting alone, tossing small pieces of old cheese to a small brown field mouse, when the prince stumbled through the trees that guided him up onto the mound.

Dreamy should have been in the mines. He should have been there all week, but Grouchy had told the supervisor that he had lungflu and no one had questioned it. He wasn't getting paid, but then they'd all lost their appetites and less food was required. Why bother trying to cook something tasty when it felt as if all the joy had been drained from the world? They were grieving and weighed down with guilt, but it was generally acknowledged that Dreamy, so much more sensitive than the aver age dwarf, was suffering the most.

He was so lost in his thoughts that he didn't hear the young man until he had staggered up the other side of the mound and was almost beside the coffin. The mouse scurried into the bushes. Dreamy reached for his knife. The stranger was tall and broad and framed in late-afternoon sunshine that danced on his dirty blond hair. He was handsome. He was also injured. Dreamy got to his feet, and moved forward quickly to catch his arm as he fell.

'Thank you,' the stranger mumbled, as Dreamy lowered him carefully to the ground. He wasn't a soldier, not from this land at any rate, and although his clothes were dirty they were made from fine fabrics. Both the hilt of his sword and his red cloak carried the same insignia. A lit torch shining through a golden crown. He was royal this one; a prince per haps. But not of this kingdom.

'Here. Drink.' He handed over his flask and the prince drank greedily from it, not caring that it was heady beer and not water. His pale skin glistened with sweat; a thick sheen that had nothing to do with the warm summer's day.

'I must find my companion,' he said, eventually. 'He's been gone for days. I think.' He frowned. 'I'm losing track of time.'

'You're injured,' Dreamy said. It was clear the man had a fever. His eyes were brilliant blue, but flecked with red and his whole body trembled. Dreamy pulled the cloak back slightly and the young man winced. A bandage of sorts was wrapped around his middle but blood had leaked through and dried, mixed with mud, on the once white linen shirt. Whatever injury lay beneath was festering. It would need attention or the dwarves would have a second lifeless royal body on their hands.

'You should come back to my cottage,' he said. 'We can—'

'What is this?' The prince's eyes narrowed as he pulled away from the dwarf and leaned over towards the glass coffin containing Snow White's perfect form. 'She's beautiful,' he said. His voice was as dry as whispering baked autumn leaves and, hearing a strange nervousness in his tone, Dreamy wondered when he'd last drunk or eaten properly. Had he lost his way to the river? How long had he been wandering?

The prince's face was so close to the glass that his sickly breath condensed on it and Snow's beautiful face was almost lost from view. He frowned again.

'Yes, she is,' Dreamy said, simply. 'She was cursed by a

crone. She seems to be neither completely dead nor alive.'
His heart broke all over again saying the words aloud.

'Cursed?' The prince's head darted round. Why did he
look so wary? 'In what way, cursed?'

'The apple,' Dreamy nodded at the perfect fruit still
gripped tightly in her small palm. 'She ate the apple.' They
both stared at the frozen girl a little longer, lost in their
individual thoughts.

'What was she like before?' the prince asked. 'Did you
know her?'

'She was beautiful,' Dreamy said. He could barely get
the words out. 'And always kind.' He wasn't ready to talk
about her yet; her wild charm, her skill on horseback, the
way she swam free and naked in the lake. Those were his
memories. They'd be razor blades on his tongue if he spoke
of them so soon.

'She was a princess,' he said. That much he could be
truthful about. There were many princesses in the stories
he'd read. Maybe none quite like Snow White, but many
he could draw on. 'A pure girl with a kind and delicate
disposition. She excelled at dancing and music. She sewed
the most ornate tapestries with silk threads. Her laugh was
like sunlight on dappled water.' He choked a little at that. It
was almost true. Her laugh was richer though; molten ore in
the heart of the rocks they battled daily. But her smile, her
smile was all nature and sunlight, and when he remembered

it she was always splashing in the pond, gently mocking them for not coming in.

'She sounds perfect.' The prince had laid down alongside the coffin, staring in. 'A true beauty.'

'She was.' Dreamy wiped away his tears and then dipped into his fictions to tell more stories of the beautiful princess who'd been cursed for her kindness. The sun slowly set, but he didn't stop. The prince didn't interrupt him, but it was only when he began to twitch and mutter that Dreamy snapped back to reality and realised how much time had passed. The stranger had fallen into a fever, no doubt caused by his wound and, collapsed on the grass, he tossed and turned in the grip of a nightmare, his eyes moving rapidly behind their lids. Dreamy tried to wake him and pull him to his feet, but he was too far gone and too heavy.

'Beauty,' the prince mumbled urgently, the rest of his sentence lost in hot breath and half words. 'Beauty.'

7

'A princess is missing'

The dwarves made him a makeshift bed beside the coffin. The cottage was too cramped and they decided the fresh, warm air would be good for him. Stumpy built him a fire and they dressed his wounds and fed him broth as the fever slowly broke. It wasn't just him who slowly recovered; the dwarves did too. They had someone to care for, someone to mend, and in doing so their hearts too mended a little as the days passed into weeks.

The prince made his home by the glass coffin and the dwarves returned to work. Each day they came back and brought bread and stew up to the mound and would sit in the dying light and talk and some times even sing. They would sing to Snow White and the prince would join in. Every day he grew stronger, and after a while they'd come back to find he'd fetched wood and water and caught animals in the forest for them to eat. He never left the mound for long though, and hardy as the dwarves were, they could see that he was falling in love with their frozen princess.

He talked to her. They heard him sometimes, his voice low and full of good humour, recounting stories of battles and jousts and balls and a glittering castle of light. He smiled and touched the glass, as if hoping she would lift her own hand and touch his from the other side. Sometimes Dreamy would just watch from the trees. The handsome prince regaling the frozen beauty with his stories, or just sitting quietly beside her and looking at her. He willed her to breathe, just as they all did. But her eyes remained lifeless and staring skywards. As the world turned and the days passed, she did not change.

'You're nearly recovered,' Dreamy said, one evening as the fire embers died down and the dwarves headed back to their cottages. 'You'll be able to return to your land soon. You must be pleased.'

'I'm not quite well enough yet,' the young prince replied, and Dreamy thought he'd never seen such a sad and handsome face as that upon which the fading firelight danced. His own heart felt heavy. Perhaps they should have made his bed inside the small cottage. Perhaps giving him so much time with their cursed princess had been stupid. Now there was more heartache ahead when the young man would have to leave her.

He didn't read before sleeping that night. There was too much tragedy and romance already surrounding them. Instead, he lay awake on the wooden table outside the cottage and stared at the stars and wished for happy endings.

It was perhaps a week later, as the cool breath of autumn swept through the forest, that they first noticed the ravens. They were sitting on the fences at the bottom of the mountain on the Dwarf Path.

'Ravens don't come out here,' Stumpy said. He didn't break his pace, but his eyes darted upwards and his voice was low. Dreamy remembered when Stumpy had been a merrier soul who'd laughed and chatted as they'd worked, but four hours stuck beneath a rock slide, his hand crushed beside him and the dead bodies of four dwarves around him in the dark had changed him. Dreamy had been part of the rescue team. It was a day he would never forget. Stumpy had been screaming for at least an hour before he passed out. When he'd woken up, he was not the same. There were some things that changed you. This was as true as a first breath and a last, and that day had killed the dwarf who had been Dreamy's best friend, even if he still walked, and talked, and mined. Perhaps one day the old Stumpy would return, but those shadows would never be entirely shaken free. Just as Dreamy would never shake off the sound of his screams.

'What are they doing here?' Stumpy kept his voice low. They were on the mountain now, and the guard would be watching. There was no love lost between those who mined and those who supervised. The men were nearly all there on punishment duties and they envied the dwarves their good health amid the dust.

'Queen's birds,' a voice came from a team marching beside them. Dreamy looked round. The leader was rough skinned and his face had a long scar running down one side. Belcher, Dreamy thought his name was. He'd been a warrior dwarf, a city dwarf. His songs were different to theirs and his team never smiled or broke ranks when they dug. Belcher's team would not have got separated and allowed one of their own to lose a hand. Had the words come from any dwarf but him, Dreamy would have laughed them off. Instead, his guts chilled.

'How do you know?' Stumpy asked. Dreamy stayed quiet. Belcher respected Stumpy. He respected how he'd changed. Dreamy wondered what Belcher might have been like decades ago before the wars and then the mines changed him.

'I hear talk. I still have friends among the soldiers. Those are charmed birds.' His mouth barely moved as he grunted out the words and all of them kept their eyes ahead. 'She *sees* through them. Watches the city. They've never left its limits before.'

'What's she looking for, do you reckon?' Dreamy was impressed with Stumpy's casual tone. He gripped his axe hard to stop his hands trembling. There was only one thing – one person – the queen could be looking for, and that was Snow White.

'You tell me, Stumpy lad,' Belcher said, wryly. 'You tell me.'

Their shift passed interminably slowly. Dreamy found a moment to tell Grouchy what had been said, but it was nothing that could be talked about in the hot, close confines they worked in. Ears were every where and Dreamy didn't know if it was his imagination or not, but it seemed as if here and there hooded eyes turned his team's way. Was their secret safe? Snow White had been friends to all the dwarves, but it was their cottage she had come to when the drinking and singing was done. Would the other teams pass that information on to the soldiers if asked? How strong was dwarf honour – and what would happen to them if Snow White was discovered? He fought the rising panic. He would take whatever fate passed their way. They had vowed to protect the princess. They had failed once – they would not fail again.

There were no ravens in the forest; that much at least was a relief. Rain was pouring heavily through the trees as they trudged home and the drops were cold and had no summer scent as they turned their faces upwards into it and scanned the branches for silent birds.

The prince had a fire lit for them and a fresh rabbit was roasting on a spit, but as the water dripped from the dwarves to the cottage floor, the meaty scent did nothing to entice them to eat.

They sat in silence for a while, sipping beer.

'Maybe it's nothing to do with us,' Breezy said. 'Maybe she just wants to make sure we're all working?'

Grouchy barely snorted in response.

'A princess is missing,' Stumpy said. 'Even if the queen thinks she's dead, she's got to make a show of looking for her. We didn't think of that.'

'Is there anything I can do?' The prince had stayed out of their conversation, but he'd been listening from the fireside.

'You should go,' Grouchy said. 'Your land needs its prince and these are our troubles. Plus, winter is coming. You can't sleep out there forever.'

Dreamy's heart stung at the words, and the thought of Snow White out on the mound in the dark in her glass coffin, the rain hammering on it. At least the prince stayed with her. At least while he was here she was rarely alone.

'Maybe in a day or two.' He turned back to the fire. 'I still need to rest.' His jaw locked and although no one would argue with Grouchy, and he was right, they knew what really kept the handsome prince in their poor cottage and up on the mound.

'A day or two longer,' Grouchy said. 'And then, my friend, you must leave. I will not have more on my conscience.'

The prince nodded and as something unspoken passed

between the two, a thought dawned on Dreamy that hadn't occurred to him before. This prince's land might not be one of the allied kingdoms. Dwarves and politics did not mix, but had Grouchy recognised the prince's crest? Would he become a prisoner, if the queen knew about him? Would they all end up in the dungeons for harbouring him? Suddenly it was all clear. And suddenly their present danger increased tenfold.

Eventually, they filled their plates with food and forced themselves to eat, but every mouthful of meat made Dreamy want to be sick. He wished he was braver. He'd always imagined himself as the hero in the adventures he'd read, but he was starting to realise that adventures in real life were far more fear than excitement. The wicked queen was coming.

And come she did.

It was as if the weather could sense the dark magic that was spreading across the forest. The temperature had dropped overnight and rain hung in half frozen droplets across the branches. Autumn had been crushed by an early winter, the browning leaves killed by the sudden cold.

Dreamy was alone when he heard the heavy wheels of a carriage on the other side of the thick trees and bushes, followed by the sharp shouts of soldiers coming to a halt. He had been building the fire so it would last all day, and was about to race to catch the others up when he stopped, his stomach turning to water, in the clearing. The prince had gone up to the mound only minutes before, a pot of hot stew to keep him warm during his vigil, and Dreamy willed him to stay away. He stared at the trees. Maybe they wouldn't find the cottage – maybe they—

'It's here somewhere.' A woman's voice; quiet but commanding. 'Cut your way through. I will speak to them *all.*' It was *her.* The queen. Snow White's step-mother.

More shouted commands and axes and swords cut into the veins of the forest, determined to clear a pathway to the cottage door. Dreamy wanted to cry. Why was he the last one here? Why not Grouchy? Or Stumpy? They were braver. They would not be so afraid. He looked around at the small tracks leading to the pond and the mound. He wanted to run. His short, thick legs trembled with the urgency. He could make it, he was sure, and be clear and at the mine before the soldiers found their way to the Dwarf Path. The soldiers would never know the ways through the forest like the dwarves did and fear concentrated the mind.

And his mind concentrated as the axes beat out a steady rhythm towards him, branches creaking as they were torn free. He *could* run. But what would happen then? They'd search the cottage. He tried to remember if there was anything incriminating in there? Something of Snow's from times gone by? Her breeches were kept somewhere. Maybe they'd find them. Chances were they'd then search the surrounding areas. The mound was well hidden but nowhere near well enough to escape a determined queen. He thought of the ravens. How much did she know already?

Ahead of him, a gap formed in the butchered trees and he glimpsed the soldiers coming forward. The Queen's Guard. He couldn't run. He knew that much. He was the only one who could save himself and his friends.

'Hello?' he called, and stepped forward, his voice innocent and wary. 'Who's there?'

'Her Majesty the Queen!' a soldier barked.

Dreamy fell to one knee and bowed his head. He waited. Finally the axes fell silent and there was only the cool breeze rustling in the trees and the clank of soldiers' metal.

'Get up, dwarf.'

'Your Majesty.' He paused for a moment in deference before standing with his head bowed. 'What an honour. What can I do for you? I live to serve.' He'd been worried that, not being a natural liar, his face would give his guilt away; but instead, as he finally glanced up, his mouth dropped open and all thought was momentarily gone. He wasn't sure what he'd been expecting. A monster? A crone?

She was beautiful. He'd *heard* she was beautiful, of course. Snow White had said as much and the soldiers at the mines made plenty of lewd jokes about the old king's luck, but Dreamy hadn't been part of the birthday ball joke – his balance hadn't been good enough to stand on another's shoulders without causing them all to collapse – so he had never seen her for himself. He hadn't thought that there could ever be anyone as beautiful as Snow White, but here was proof otherwise.

Where Snow's hair was dark and thick, the queen's was white blonde and like a sheet of silk down her back. Her eyes angled upwards like a cat's. He noticed that beneath them were dark shadows. He felt terrified and full of pity all at once. Guilt could drive a person mad, he was sure of it.

'The princess is missing,' she said curtly. 'I know how much she likes to socialise with you... people.' She looked at the cottage and its surrounds as if the idea of spending any time in such a place was her idea of hell. 'If any of you have caused her any harm, then we will find out.'

'No dwarf would hurt her!' Dreamy exclaimed. 'We love the princess. Your Majesty knows that. But we haven't seen her for days. We thought perhaps she was caught up in business at the castle, and we're no longer allowed in the castle... so...' He let the sentence drift off to a natural end. It was this queen who had banished them, after all.

'Please,' he dropped his bag and ran to the cottage door, pulling it open – he hoped not too dramatically. 'Search our house. Please. Dwarf honour is at stake. Search the house and then I will help you hunt for her anywhere you ask. As will my brothers.'

She stared at him for a long moment and his heart was in

his mouth. If they did search the cottage then Snow White's breeches would be found and they would be done for. But if he hadn't offered this woman would have insisted. It was a dangerous bluff, but it was also all he had.

'You've heard none of the other dwarves talking about her?' the queen asked.

'No, your Majesty. But I will listen harder, I promise you.'

'Make sure you do. My ravens will travel further into the forest soon.' She looked at the trees around them as if they were an army standing against her. 'Then we'll find her, however well she's hidden.'

Dreamy said nothing, not sure he could trust himself to speak, but the queen was lost in her own thoughts.

'I just need to know,' she said softly, to the trees and the breeze perhaps, but not to man or dwarf. 'I'll go mad if I never *know*.'

She turned and walked back along the new path to her carriage and after a second or two snapped her fingers. The Queen's Guard gave Dreamy one more suspicious glare and then followed her. The trees and bushes were already knotting themselves back together and the dwarf was pleased to hear one small exclamation of pain as a bramble caught on a passing soldier's cheek.

'To the next one!' The queen commanded, her voice carrying easily to the clearing. 'And then to the mines.'

Dreamy waited until the horses had been spurred on,

and the roll of the carriage's wheels was no longer audible, before he allowed his legs to give way beneath him. He sat trembling on a tree stump, his breathing ragged and harsh. For a while he thought perhaps that they might come back – that this was an elaborate ruse to lull him into a sense of calm only to return, declare him a traitor and drag him to the dungeons – but no wheels or horses returned and as his panic finally left him and his skin cooled, Dreamy knew what he had to do. There was no time to wait for the others. Their shift wouldn't be finished for many long hours yet, and by then anything could have happened. The ravens might spy Snow White from above or – and although it was a terrible thought he knew it was possible – one of their own kind might betray them. They'd kept Snow White a secret, but all the dwarves knew that his team were her favourites.

As soon as his legs were steady he went up to the mound, fighting the urge to run and instead moving cautiously, checking around him for signs of soldiers or spies. The dense forest, however, was empty and each of his own footsteps was too loud as he made his way along the familiar route and up to the sunny peak.

The prince was sitting with his head bowed as Dreamy arrived. He didn't look over, but continued to stare at the beautiful face within the glass coffin.

'I know you all want me to go,' he said. 'And I should go. For all your sakes. But I can't. I can't leave her.' A single tear trickled down his perfect face. 'I think it would kill me.'

'You have to take her with you,' Dreamy said. 'You have to take her back to your kingdom.'

'What?' The prince looked up.

'I'll come with you to the border. She's not safe here.'

'But your kingdom and mine...'

'I know,' Dreamy said. There was a war between them. Of course. He had been naïve. Not anymore. Dreamy was growing up fast today. 'But you must keep her safe until her father returns. Until we can figure out what the curse is and how to lift it.'

'And then I will marry her and our two kingdoms will be unified at last.' The prince's shoulders were straightening already.

'I'll prepare the cart,' Dreamy said. 'The Queen's Guard are searching the dwarf cottages. If we move now and stay away from those paths then we have a chance of getting out of the forest and away from the clutches of the castle by nightfall. But we have to move now.'

8

'A lost prince and a cursed princess'

They had worked quickly, and were on the road within an hour. Dreamy had cleared the evidence from the cottage and then they lifted the coffin onto the back of the dusty wooden cart and covered it with an old blanket before surrounding it with firewood and bags of potatoes and old vegetables in the hope that it would pass at least a brief inspection. They'd harnessed the dwarves' old, tired pony, that had done no more than the occasional trip to market for years, and the forest had let them through.

The first half an hour had been a tense affair until they were away from the main tracks and onto rockier, less well used terrain. The dwarf led them, the pony responding best to his familiar clicks and tugs on the rein, and the prince brought up the rear. They didn't speak much and the prince didn't mind. The quiet meant the dwarf was focused and on the look out for danger. For his own part, he kept one hand on the hilt of his sword, hidden beneath his cloak which was turned inside out and covered in mud to darken its colours. He might look like a thief, he'd decided, but he certainly didn't look like a travelling prince.

He rested one hand on the cart and wished Snow White's frozen face wasn't hidden from both him and the sunlight. He hated the thought of that stinking blanket covering her like a shroud. She was too beautiful and tragic and perfect for that. Dreamy was right, she was safer this way, but he didn't have to like it. There was nothing noble or regal about being transported in fear, on the back of a dirty cart. Maybe when he got back to the castle he'd change the story. For her sake, as much as his. He remembered his injury and all that came *before* he'd wandered and found the dwarves. He shuddered. There would be a few stories that would have to be changed. But still, the dwarves had saved his life and brought him *this* sleeping beauty, and for that he would forever be grateful. When he was home he would send riches back to them as a reward.

In the absence of his missing companion the prince might never have found his way out of this kingdom and back to his own, but the little dwarf up ahead seemed never to be lost, instead steadily picking his way along the narrow paths and choosing between two or three at a crossroads with a confident ease. The prince was glad. Now that he had secured his princess he couldn't wait to get home. He'd had enough of adventures. The castle of light, jousts and dancing; that's all he wanted. His prince's life again. He shivered with pleasure at the thought. This mining kingdom was rough and brutal compared to his own, where courtly manners and beautiful things were treasured, and music and society balls filled the evenings. His heart ached to be there with his exquisite princess by his side. He would have his father scour the land for the finest magicians there were, to undo whatever curse had been laid upon her. He would save her and she would love him as he loved her and they would live happily ever after.

His feet trudged on in pace with the pony that might not have been swift but was at least steady, and after a few hours, Dreamy began to hum. Although the tune was coarse and clumsy compared to the minuets they played at home, he'd grown used to the dwarf songs, and he joined in. Maybe there were parts of the dwarf life he would miss. The brotherhood. The unspoken friendships and loyalties. Both things that were so hard to find when born of royal blood.

'You're not singing it right.'

The gruff voice came from behind them, and the prince turned fast, drawing his sword.

'You could take a man's eye out with that,' Grouchy said,

emerging from the bushes and onto the rocky track. 'A taller man's eye, admittedly.'

'What are you doing here?' Dreamy asked as he rushed towards the older dwarf. 'Are you angry? I couldn't wait. I'm sorry. I thought this was for the best. There was no time to—'

'Stop babbling.' Grouchy swatted at the air as if Dreamy's words were irritating flies. 'You did the right thing. We heard about the queen's hunt at the mines when the next shift came in, and as you hadn't showed up I came looking for you. Saw your note in the chimney.' He slapped Dreamy on the shoulder. 'That was good thinking. Where Snow White used to leave us messages.' He nodded at the prince. 'But I thought I'd come and keep you company. Dwarves aren't solitary creatures and it'll be a long walk back when these two are safe.'

'Thank you, Grouchy.' Dreamy looked as if he might burst into tears of relief, and the prince wondered at how little he really knew these hardy men. A fear of walking alone was not one he'd imagined in someone who was finding his way so well through the forest. 'It's good to have you along,' he said, and smiled. 'Now teach us how to sing it properly.'

They sang quietly together, the prince daydreaming of home and Snow White dancing at his side, and day slowly shifted into afternoon and then into the strange grey of dusk. Finally, they fell silent and walked by the flame of a single torch. They were tired and their legs ached, but they would walk through the night if that's what it took to get to the edge of the forest. To be far enough from the castle to be safe.

As it turned out that was what it took. The prince was sure that he dozed as he walked for a while, suddenly jolted out of his reverie by either Dreamy or Grouchy handing him some water and a piece of hard bread to chew on. The hours were endless and the uneven ground beneath his boots meant he stumbled painfully as much as he walked. The hardy pony should have been dead hours ago but it maintained the same steady pace, forcing them all to keep up. The night was relentless. The prince began to wonder if they were all cursed on a journey that would never end. He tried to focus on thoughts of home or Snow White's perfect beauty but his mind kept being dragged down into other, darker memories which played out like nightmares. Running through a different forest in fear for his life. A couple of times he cried out, and Grouchy took his arm, gruffly waking him, but it was hard to tell where the boundary between fantasy and reality lay.

At last the pitch darkness that gripped them fractured with shards of grey and then yellow and orange as dawn broke. The prince could have cried with relief. Exhaustion had taken them all prisoner and was torturing their every step, but the trees were definitely thinning and the track widening into a proper road. They were near the edge of the forest. They would have rest soon. He was about to burst into a laugh of relief when the pony suddenly started and reared up, whinnying in terror and sending the cart tilting up and the contents spilling out onto the road.

The prince felt as if he was moving through sludge as he grabbed for the cart, missing completely and falling sideways to find himself attacked by tumbling vegetables. The dwarves tugged at the pony's reins trying to calm her and then finally, there was a quiet stillness.

'What the fuck happened?' Grouchy said.

'It's just a mouse.' Dreamy was crouched in the road. 'Look.' The prince hauled himself to his aching feet and limped over. A small field mouse, a scar cutting down its back, was merrily cleaning itself in the middle of their path. It paused and looked up curiously at them, completely unafraid. Dreamy laughed a little. 'It's just a mouse.'

'Look at the mess. I'm sure that wheel isn't sitting right. This is going to—'

'What's that sound?' The prince frowned.

'What sound? Dreamy looked round, suddenly peering through the gaps in the trees, no doubt for the arrival of soldiers.

'Listen.' The prince turned back towards the broken cart. It had come from that direction. He heard it again. A cough. 'That.'

The little mouse scurried between their legs and over to the glass coffin which lay, half spilled, still covered with the dirty blanket, on the road. They all turned and watched as he sniffed around a little and then nibbled on a fallen potato. The cough came again. Light and feminine.

'The coffin,' the prince whispered. 'It's coming from the coffin.'

The prince reached it first, the dwarves right behind him and between the three of them they care fully laid it out on the road and pulled the blanket away. From inside, Snow White looked blearily up at them, the small piece of apple that had been trapped in her throat now lying on her chest.

'The crash dislodged it!' Dreamy cried. 'She hadn't swallowed it! It was stuck half way!'

'Get her out of there,' Grouchy grumbled. 'The clasps on the side. Undo them.'

The prince was already working at them. Was this a dream? Were they still walking through the night and this was just an illusion that would shatter at any moment? Could she really be awake? He'd wished for this moment since he'd first laid eyes on her, and now here it was, out of the blue.

The glass lid came away, and he leaned forward.

'Who are you?' Her voice was husky and cracked a little.

'Shh,' he said, and before he could stop himself, he leaned down and kissed her. Her lips were every bit as soft and sweet as he'd imagined them to be. He lingered for a few seconds enjoying the feel of her body heat rising from the confines of the glass, and then he pulled back. She looked up at him, breathless.

'I'm the man you're going to marry.'

She sat up suddenly and looked down at her dress and then at the apple in her hand. 'Um... what's going on?'

'It's a long story,' Dreamy said. 'Let's get a fire going and we'll tell you. First,' he leaned in towards the apple, 'we should throw that away.'

Out of nowhere, the little brown mouse scurried up Dreamy's arm and onto the edge of the glass side, standing on his rear legs, with his whiskers twitching. He leaned towards the fruit.

'No, no,' Snow White said. 'We need to put it somewhere safe. Otherwise the animals will eat it.' She looked at the prince. 'Have you got a pouch or something?'

'Of course.' He took the apple and the small bite she'd coughed up and put them in his money bag. She was beautiful and also kind. The dwarves had been right. This was magical. It was love. It had to be.

They made camp in a small clearing at the side of the road and in the glow of the fire, the two dwarves and the prince told her all that had happened since the crone gave her the apple. The prince let Dreamy tell her of his vigil and how he'd sat beside her as she lay there somewhere between life and death, through all the days and nights. When they were done, she turned and looked up at him. 'You were going to keep me safe?' she asked.

'I'm still going to keep you safe,' he said, wrapping one arm around her and pulling her close. On the other side of the fire, the two dwarves beamed with happiness. 'Marry me and come back to my kingdom. You will be the brightest jewel in the crown of my palace of light. You will never want for anything, I promise you.'

She looked into the fire and his heart raced with his love for her. 'Please be my wife,' he said. 'I've been searching for you all my life. This is true love. I knew it when I first laid eyes on you.' He could feel heat rising on his face; embarrassment and excitement. She had to say yes. She had to. Surely she must feel something for him too.

'A lost prince and a cursed princess,' Dreamy said. 'It's so romantic. Like something from one of the story books you gave me.'

'The queen tried to kill me,' she said softly.

'And she'll try again if she gets the chance,' Grouchy said. 'She's wicked, that one.'

The seconds passed like hours as she continued gazing into the crackling flames, the light from which licked at her face as if it too wanted to touch her beauty. What was she thinking? Her expression was as unreadable as it had been while she was frozen. He was rushing her, he knew, but what else could he do? If he took her back unmarried his father would probably try and put a stop to it. He wanted to arrange his son's marriage himself. He'd *seen* some of the women his father would choose and they weren't for him. But to return already married, to a royal princess, was something he wouldn't be able to put aside. And once he'd calmed down, he'd realise that the warring could end and a new alliance could be made. Snow White's kingdom had mines and metal. His father would want both.

'Yes,' she said. The first time she said the word so quietly it was almost lost in the crackle of the fire.

'What?'

'Yes.' She looked up at him. 'Yes, I will marry you. Why not?'

The dwarves were on their feet and hugging the breath from Snow White before her answer had sunk in, and then his hand was being shaken so hard by Grouchy that he could barely speak.

'Enough, enough!' She broke away, laughing. 'Let's do it straight away. Tomorrow. Why wait?' Her face was shining with a wild excitement and he leaned forward to kiss her again. Her lips brushed his and then she pulled back. 'Not until our wedding night,' she said. 'I'm a princess, after all.'

The prince's heart almost burst. Beautiful, kind and demure. Exactly what he'd always wanted. A perfect princess. After everything that had happened *before* his injury he'd lost faith that such a creature existed, but after all his trials, the loss of his companion and the days of nightmarish delirium, here she was.

'Tomorrow,' he said, grinning like a child. 'We'll wed tomorrow!'

9

'Let's get married'

Dreamy and Grouchy had mended the cart and reloaded it as the young couple slept. The dwarves hadn't slept much, guarding the fire and their precious human company throughout the night, but they were both happy in their work. 'Sometimes things happen for a reason,' Grouchy said. 'If the crone hadn't given her the apple, who knows if these two would have found each other.'

'Have you been reading one of my story books?' Dreamy teased as they harnessed the pony. 'You're sounding almost romantic.'

'Fuck off with you,' Grouchy said, but a small blush crept across his gnarly face. Dreamy smiled. It was a happy ending. They'd be able to leave tonight knowing she was finally safe. The weight of their guilt had been lifted. There would be no awful fate awaiting them for not being able to keep their word.

'I'll miss her though,' he added. It was true. Snow White was a light in their otherwise dull lives, and as the kingdom was sinking into the dark mire of the queen's magic, there would be very little pleasure to see them through the winter and to the king's eventual return. She had always been there for them, and now she would become part of another kingdom.

'She'll be back,' Grouchy said. 'I've got a feeling in my bones about it.'

'At least she'll be safe and happy.'

They smiled at each other and finally woke the sleeping beauties.

After the chill of the dawn the day broke into sunshine; a final war cry of summer, or perhaps just that the queen's winter hadn't stretched this far out into the kingdom yet. Either way, the sun was warm on their backs as they finally broke free of the forest.

'Look,' the prince said. Ahead, where the land dipped into a valley, a higgledy piggeldy town was visible, smoke rising from chimneys as the day started. The royal crest flew from the top of the town hall, the bright colours standing proud against the white stone of the buildings and the blue sky above. Next to the pennant was a smaller one, and although none of them could make it out exactly they knew it was the queen's mark.

'Not short of ambition then, your step-mother.' Grouchy muttered as the road widened beneath them.

'No,' Snow said. 'She's certainly unique.' She was holding Dreamy's hand and he gave it a squeeze.

'Well, she can't hurt you now,' he said. 'You're safe from her.'

'I suppose I am.' Her voice was soft but sadness gave it weight.

'We can't be sure of that until you're across the border,' Grouchy added.

'There's a chapel,' the prince cried. 'There! I can see the steeple!' He smiled down at Snow White. 'Let's get married.'

Dreamy was as close to tears as dwarves got before Grouchy had even started to walk Snow White down the aisle. It hadn't taken them long to find the priest, and even though he'd raised his eyebrows at the young couple's urgency to marry – no doubt suspecting it a sudden necessity rather than a romantic act – it had only taken a couple of the prince's gold coins to persuade him to get dressed and meet them at the chapel. It was still quite early and the streets were relatively quiet. Dreamy had picked the last of summer's wild flowers and threaded them together into a headband for Snow White, the pinks and reds picking out the lilac hue of her beautiful eyes. The prince had beaten at the door of a dressmaker's until they too had opened up and their initial anger evaporated when they sold a fine white dress to the beautiful girl and her beau.

Snow hadn't stopped laughing all morning; a wild carefree sound that Dreamy normally associated with some crazy adventure or prank, but as she went with Grouchy to get rooms at the inn and change into her dress she became calmer. It was her wedding day, after all. It needed to be taken seriously. Even by one so wild as Snow White.

Dreamy went to the chapel with the prince and they waited quietly with the priest for her to arrive. It was no ornate royal church, but the small building had a charm of its own. The high arched windows were clear of decoration. The cool air sang with the scent of the lilies that filled huge vases on either side of the small altar. The wooden pews were plain but well varnished. It was a peaceful place, Dreamy decided. A good place. He couldn't imagine a royal wedding, with all its sumptuous glory, could be more meaningful.

He remembered the parades and processions when the king married his ice queen. The kingdom had been filled with pageantry for days, and what did that marriage have? A man in thrall to a beautiful woman, perhaps, but that was not a union of love. No woman became that wicked when she'd fallen in love. But then, his knowledge of these things was limited. Dwarf women were rare and always died in child birth, producing at least five small babies at once. No dwarf ever knew their mother. Waiting in the chapel he said a quiet prayer for his own lost mother. He didn't believe in any of the gods, but neither did he know what else to do with his sudden maudlin thoughts. This was a happy day. Snow White would be blessed with children and she would know them and love them. Her life would be perfect. It *had* to be.

Finally, the doors opened and Grouchy and Snow White began the walk to the altar. There was no organ, but Grouchy was singing a dwarf song, a slow end of the day marching tune. His deep voice echoed and Dreamy's throat tightened as he watched them pass him. Like a true princess, Snow White kept her head up and focused on her waiting husband ahead, and Dreamy thought that dressed in the simple white shift, and with her dark hair flowing free around her shoulders beneath the crown of flowers, he'd never seen her looking so beautiful.

Sunlight cut through the church, dust dancing in it like fireflies, and framed the pair as they quietly took their vows. The prince, so tall and handsome, didn't take his eyes from the princess throughout the whole ceremony, and when the priest finally declared that he could kiss the bride, even he smiled happily as the young couple did as they were bid. There was something special in the moment, something magical, and outside birds began to sing.

They were man and wife. Prince and princess. And they would live happily ever after.

* * *

'I think we should keep it,' the prince said. 'As a souvenir of how we met.' He stroked the glass coffin on the back of the cart.

'Technically, we didn't meet that way,' Snow White said. 'I wasn't exactly there. But if it has sentimental value to you then why not. I love that the dwarves made it for me. That they didn't bury me.' She smiled at Grouchy. 'You saved me, really.'

The day was getting hotter and after a quick wedding breakfast at the inn, the dwarves were getting ready to say their farewells and head back into the forest. Dreamy wasn't looking forward to it. It had all happened so fast and now Snow White was heading off to live in a completely different kingdom. It was for her own good, he knew, but he wished he and Grouchy could stay too. Not that it was possible. Dwarves belonged in the mines, and if they didn't return the rest of their team would suffer.

'Here,' the prince reached into his money pouch and pulled out several gold coins. 'To replace your cart and pony. If you don't mind us taking them.' He stroked the pony's mane. 'She's worked hard. She deserves a good retirement.'

'Then you take her,' Grouchy said. 'You'll give her a better life than we can.' The prince pressed the coins into Dreamy's protesting hands. He could smell sweet apples on the metal from where they'd shared space with the crone's cursed gift to Snow. Was this now poisoned money, he wondered. Why did that thought give him such a chill? He shook it away. Grouchy was right. He spent far too much time with his head in books. His imagination was getting too able to carry him away.

'But we should buy ourselves some horses to ride home on,' the prince said. 'I can't walk back into the castle. I need a proper horse and mine is lost.'

'Let me get changed first,' Snow White said. 'I want my normal clothes on.' She reached up and kissed her husband on his nose. 'Wait here.' The prince blushed and Dreamy felt better. Money could be washed. There was nothing tainted here.

The prince had bought her several fine dresses from the seamstress, but when she emerged she was wearing her riding breeches and white shirt, and her hair was pulled back in an untidy knot. Natural beauty shone from her and she took the prince's hand and dragged him to the horse merchant. The prince looked surprised at what she was wearing, but it made Dreamy smile. It was her, their princess, earthy and passionate and back with them again.

After picking out a fine steed for himself, the prince chose Snow White a grey pony with plaits in its mane and that pranced around the corral as if it were dancing. She laughed and shook her head, her hair shining in the sunlight.

'That's no horse for me. I've always ridden a stallion. Let me choose.' She pushed past him and walked along the line of stalls until she reached the furthest. Inside, a black beast pawed at the ground, eyes burning with rage at his captivity.

'This one,' she said.

'Are you sure?' Dreamy peered over the edge of the door. 'He looks a little dangerous, even for you.'

'That's no lady's horse,' the prince said.

'I'm with yer man,' the horse dealer cut in, spitting tobacco into the sawdust. 'That one won't break.'

'Let's see, shall we?' Ignoring them all, Snow White undid the gate and stepped inside the stable. The horse stamped his feet and shook his head, snorting angrily, but the slim girl stood beside him and stroked his neck, whispering quietly into the beast's ear. After a moment, she gripped the thick mane and pulled herself effortlessly onto his back.

The beast reared and snarled but she stayed on, urging him out of the confined space and into the sunlight. She laughed as he tried to throw her, her face glowing with the sheer energy of life.

'He's going to throw you!' the prince cried out. 'Get down!'

'I'm no chicken!' Snow White called back. 'Just watch me.'

And watch they did. It was all they could do as the horse and rider took to the corral and began their battle for command. Dreamy was in awe. She was so fearless; so alive in the moment. She had her father's strength and her mother's grace and beauty. She and the horse were as one.

'She rides like a man,' the prince said, as they watched her finally tame the beast to a canter, her thighs controlling him as they turned this way and that, her hair falling free from the loose bun. 'What woman rides like a man?'

'Oh, I don't think there's another woman like our Snow White in all the kingdoms,' Grouchy said, pride clear in his voice. 'You're a lucky man.'

'That horse is more powerful than mine,' the prince said. He looked a little stunned and Dreamy squeezed his arm.

'She's a force of nature. You'll get used to her.'

'I suppose I shall.'

The horse came to a halt in front of them and whinnied as Snow White dismounted. She was breathless and flushed with excitement and she flung her arms around the prince's neck. 'What an amazing ride.' Her voice was so sweet and warm that Dreamy could see the prince melting in it.

'If you want the horse, he's yours.'

'We should leave,' Grouchy said. 'You'll be safe here and the border is only a mile or so north.'

'Don't go yet.' Snow White turned, crestfallen.

'But it's your wedding day. Tonight's your wedding night. It's a time for you two to be alone.'

Dreamy blushed and kicked at the earth. Sex wasn't something dwarves had a lot to do with.

'But that's tonight,' Snow White said. 'Leave tonight

then. Today's our wedding day so celebrate with us. I know what.' She grinned. 'Let's have a beer.' She strode off ahead, and then turned, one hand on her trousered hip. 'Come on, what are you waiting for?'

The prince was staring after her, dumbfounded.

'She's probably just nervous,' Dreamy said, suddenly feeling as if he needed to make an excuse for her behaviour. He'd read that women got nervous before their wedding nights. He didn't really want to contemplate why.

'Yes, that's probably it,' the prince said, and finally they followed her.

10

'What was his father going to say?'

It was not quite as he'd expected. In fact, it was not at all as he'd expected. The prince felt somewhat dazed and confused by his new wife's behaviour. His head was in a whirl, although that could have been the beer. There had been a lot of beer, and as he watched his wife dancing enthusiastically with Dreamy in the middle of the tavern, he realised that not only could she outride him, she could outdrink him too.

It was hot and humid in the bar and although it had been early afternoon when they'd arrived, it was now dark outside. The day had lived up to its promise and given them the last of the summer, but it meant that men who'd spent hours sweating in the baking heat were now crammed into the small space. In the corner a fiddler was playing furiously and several couples joined the dwarf and the princess in a reel, whirling each other this way and that in a clumsy over enthusiastic frenzy. The prince could feel his hair curling with the moisture and he took another sip of his beer. His time with the dwarves had accustomed him to the bitter taste but he longed for the fine wines of home. Elegant dinners. Polite dances.

The party had started when Snow White had drained her third beer in a drinking competition with two merchants and then demanded they both dance with her as her prize. They were, of course, delighted, and he had no recourse but to give them his nod. After that, the whole inn became infected with her energy and soon word had spread through out the town that a celebration was in progress and more revellers poured in. That had been several hours ago, and now night had fallen outside but the dancers showed no hint of slowing down. He wished they would. He hated the way his shirt clung to his skin and, more than that, he hated the way his new bride's shirt clung to hers so every man in the room could see the lines of her body. What was she wearing a man's shirt for anyway?

'We should leave soon.'

The prince looked down to see Grouchy standing beside him.

'And you two should be getting to your bridal bed.'

'My bride doesn't seem too keen,' the prince said. 'She's

more interested in dancing and drinking.'

'Well, she's always loved both of those, that's true. But she's also been through a terrible time. She seems a little wilder than normal, I can't deny it, but what can you really expect? And this is her wedding day. Wild and happy have always gone hand in hand with Snow White.' He slapped the prince's arm lightly. 'Don't you worry, she can do serene and lady like when she has to. It just doesn't come naturally to her.'

'She's... she's not how Dreamy described her. When she was in the box. When we'd talk about her.'

'Ha!' Grouchy snorted. 'Why do you think we call him Dreamy? He lives in storybooks that one. Perhaps thinking of her as she really is was too painful.' The dwarf paused. 'But she is the kindest, most beautiful person I have ever met. Look at the joy she instils in strangers. It's a rare gift, she has, the ability to make people smile. She'll make you very happy.'

The prince watched his beautiful dancing wife as the crowd applauded her. 'Yes, she will,' he said. 'Yes, she will.'

It was late by the time they said farewell to the dwarves and headed up to their bedroom. All Snow White's good humour had dampened into tears as she squeezed each of the two goodbye, and she had insisted on watching until they had long disappeared into the night. He'd taken her hand and led her up to the bedroom where he'd just held her for a while as she'd cried, and he found her tears were something of a relief. She was helpless like this, her face pressed into his chest. He felt like a prince again. The man who'd saved her from imprisonment in the box. She was his perfect princess. Her breath was hot on his neck and her full breasts were pressed into his chest. His heart beat faster and he swallowed hard as desire crept up on him, warmth flooding his body. He'd imagined this moment so many times before, and now it was finally here.

He'd had his share of serving girls and even several of the ladies of the court at home, but never had he longed for a woman as he had Snow White. He'd studied the curves of her body as she'd laid in her glass coffin and he'd dreamed of touching her and feeling her respond beneath him. His breath became more uneven and hers steadied as he stiffened against her. Finally she looked up at him.

'Don't worry,' he said. 'I won't hurt you.'

'I'll go and...' she hesitated, 'and get myself ready. There's a washroom in the corridor.'

He put a finger over her lips, not wanting to sully the moment with talk of hygiene and human sweat. That was for base lust and servants, not for a prince and his princess. He kissed her, and despite the beer and roasted meat she'd devoured so enthusiastically throughout the evening, she still tasted sweet, and her mouth was warm, wet and inviting.

She picked up the new nightdress he'd bought her and when she left the room he quickly stripped and washed with the water in the jug and basin on the small table. It was icy cold and made him shiver but even an entire freezing ocean wouldn't be able to douse his desire. He throbbed with the thought of possessing her, his qualms about her wildness for gotten as he thought of her ripe body. There were no princesses in any of the kingdoms so beautiful. A dark memory came to him and he shook it away before it could cling to his skin and make him wilt. That adventure was done and, foul as it had been, it had led him to this happy conclusion. He was married. He would unite the kingdoms. His father would have steel in the land and keep his enemies at bay, and he and Snow White would live happily ever after and produce fit and healthy heirs. Not too soon, he hoped. He'd seen how quickly women's bodies changed after childbirth and he wanted to enjoy his wife's for as long as possible before they settled into domesticity and he went back to relieving himself with a mistress. He wasn't kidding himself that there wouldn't be other women – some of his needs were more base than others and he couldn't imagine treating Snow White that way – but she was beautiful and he wanted to make love to her for years to come.

Snow White. Purity. Perfection. He didn't even know her real name, and neither did he want to. He blew out the candles around the room, leaving only the red glow of the crackling fire that was slowly dying in the grate. He slid beneath the sheets and waited, resting on one arm, his heart thumping in anticipation.

After what seemed like an age, she finally returned. The soft, sheer fabric caught around her legs as she moved towards the bed, hinting at what was hidden beneath. Was she nervous he wondered? Her eyes were dark coals in the dim light, and they gave nothing away. Her hair hung loose and thick around her shoulders.

'Come to bed,' he said. His voice choked slightly. However strange he'd found some of her behaviour, he was in no doubt that he wanted her. He pulled the sheets back, but she didn't move. 'Don't be nervous.'

'I'm not,' she said, and her hands went to the neck of the fabric and she undid the delicate ties there. The nightdress slid from her, floating to the floor like gossamer. She swayed slightly; a flower caught in a breeze, and he realised she was still a bit drunk. Had she needed to drink because she was nervous? Maybe that was it? She stepped forward out of the shadow and into the glow of the fire. He'd expected her to get into the bed still dressed – he'd half expected her clothing to stay tangled on her throughout, especially the first time. But instead she stood before him gloriously naked. He couldn't stop staring. Her skin was smooth and her full breasts sat high, generous dark pink nipples erect in the evening air. Generous. Despite her slim frame, it was the word that best fit her. Generous. Luxurious. Decadent. Her head fell forward slightly, her hair tumbling across her face, and she held her arms out wide and spun slowly round.

'How do you like your princess?' She looked over her shoulder at him, her full lips slightly parted, her eyes challenging him from behind her hair.

'I like her very much,' he said. Her arse was round and firm. His balls ached and he throbbed with wanting to feel her from the inside; to ride her as she'd ridden that stallion. To *tame* her. 'Now come to bed.'

'Say please,' she purred.

This wasn't how he'd expected it to be at all. Where was his nervous bride? Why did he suddenly feel as if he were the one being seduced? He was the prince, the warrior; he'd faced things no man should ever see, but he suddenly felt weak. His mouth dried as lust overwhelmed him. 'Please.' The word was barely more than a whisper.

She smiled, the cat with the cream and came onto the bed on all fours, crawling towards him. He reached for her and pulled her close, one hand in her hair, his mouth seeking hers. Her tongue danced with his, and the air was filled with their hot breathing. His hand reached for her breast, feeling the warm weight of it and rolling her nipple hard between his fingers. She moaned slightly and bit down on his lip. He gasped, and in that moment she pulled away, leaving only the night air caressing his skin.

'What are you...?' The question faded as her tongue ran down his chest and into the coarse hairs at the base of his belly. Her soft, dark mane trailed behind her mouth like feathers over his skin. He couldn't stand it. He was going to explode.

Her tongue flicked over the tip of his erection and he gasped again, reaching for her hair to pull her mouth over him, but she moved on, her mouth exploring lower, running through the crevices between his thighs. What was she doing? How? Sensation flooded through his body sending electric tingles to each of his extremities and then, just as he thought his pleasure couldn't get more tantalising, she took him in her mouth.

All thought left him as he thrust deep into her hot throat, her tongue running up and down the length of him as her wet mouth embraced him. He hardened, his balls contracting. It had been too long. He wasn't going to last.

She broke free and straddled him, on her knees before him, a vision of earthy, animal beauty. She was no perfect princess, he knew that now. He didn't quite know what she was, this creature before him. He didn't understand her at all. What kind of royal family was this, where the king's treasure, his only daughter, could learn such tricks that never came until the marriage bed, and even then were more to the taste of wenches than ladies?

He grabbed her hips, wanting to pull her down on him.

'No,' she said, her voice all husky breath; a wolf in the forest. She pushed him back on the bed. 'Your turn first.'

Her tongue dipped into his mouth briefly, she flashed him a wild smile, and then she was over him, her legs either side of his head. She moaned as she pushed herself against his tongue and he was over whelmed by the heady, musky taste of her. He looked up as she grew wetter and hotter in his mouth. One hand gripped the headboard, and the other teased one nipple of her perfect breasts. Her head was thrown back as she rode him, lost in her own imaginings. She was a stranger. Someone he didn't know. He pushed his tongue further inside her and felt her squirm, the firm muscles in her thighs tightening around him. She was panting, loud and raw, moving closer to a climax.

She was riding *him*. The thought hit him, and his passion and anger and confusion roared into one movement. He pulled her down and rolled on top of her. Her eyes, still hazy with lust, widened with surprise. He pinned her down on the bed, his arms blocking hers, and pushed hard into her, waiting for the moment of give. None came, just tight heat and wetness and an upward thrust from beneath him. He buried his head in her hair and fucked her hard, until finally he exploded inside her, crying out with the release.

They lay side by side in the growing dark as their sweat cooled on their skin. The prince didn't pull her close to him and neither did she move. There was only the sound of their slowing breathing and the flutter of wings on the windowsill outside.

'Must be an owl,' Snow White said, eventually. Her voice was soft and small. Guilty. He rolled onto his side, away from her, and stared into the gloom. His jaw tightened. What was it with women and deception? Why could they never be as they appeared?

'Look, I...' The bed creaked as she turned to face his back.

'It wasn't your first time.' It wasn't a question. He knew it as fact. It was obvious from everything she'd done. He'd been deceived.

'It's not like... there was only... it wasn't like you think.'

He didn't move. He didn't speak and the silence became interminable. He squeezed his eyes shut and wished sleep would come.

'I'm sorry,' she said, eventually, and rolled the other way, pulling her knees up under her chin. The air between them was cold; a few inches and yet vast as an ocean. How had it come to this so quickly? And why had that stupid dwarf not just told him the truth about her? Would he have loved her anyway if she hadn't been such a shock?

What was his father going to say?

By morning, he had made up his mind.

After a fitful hour or so's sleep he woke to find her lying

on her side watching him, her dark hair spread out on the pillow behind her. As ever, for a moment, he was lost in her beauty.

'I've been thinking,' she said. She chewed her rose bud bottom lip slightly, with her perfect white teeth. 'We could just pretend we never got married. I'd understand. I wouldn't say anything. I could go back to the dwarves. Or somewhere else. You can go back to your kingdom. No one would ever have to know. I should have said...'

He reached a hand out and stroked her face and then leaned forward and kissed her. 'It's okay.'

'But you...?'

'I said it's okay.' He moved closer, pulling her ripe body next to his. 'You're so beautiful,' he whispered, as he felt himself react to the feel of her. 'So perfect. I could never let you go.'

He rolled her under him, taking control, and when she tried to speak he silenced her words with his mouth on hers. She was his princess. She was *his*. And she would stay that way.

11

'Wine never solved anyone's problems'

The raven had flown all night, and although it was morning the castle was still shrouded in darkness from the heavy black rain clouds that hung thick across the land. Candles flickered here and there in the gloom, and as the wind and rain from the open windows gusted in, their flames went out one by one.

Lilith was cold but she didn't care. A hot fire burned inside as she sat on her lone throne, her knees pulled up under her chin, and stared at the small mirrors which relayed all the bird had seen. She watched it over and over. Snow White and the handsome prince in bed. Alive and breathing. The wine glass was tight in her hands. If her great-grandmother had still been there she would have tutted and taken it from her. Wine in the morning was no good for kings or paupers, she'd have said. Wine never solved anyone's problems. Have some milk instead. She took another gulp and her head swam.

The wind howled outside, lashing rain across the tower's marble floor as thunder growled in the sky, and on the windowsill the raven shivered. She snapped her fingers and the images stopped. The raven flew away, released from her charm for now. She'd seen enough. She'd seen far too much.

She got to her feet, her legs stiff and aching, and headed to the small room at the back. Her head was a jumble of drunken thoughts and as she thought once more of Snow White and the handsome prince being so base together in that cheap country inn, lightning flashed bright. The tower was in the eye of the storm. The queen *was* the eye of the storm.

As she touched and caressed her magical items, hoping to find some calm in them, she raged against her own stupidity. She'd been to that dwarf cottage. She recognised the little man the raven had shown her, standing at the back of the church as Snow White had wed her weak chinned prince. He'd lied to her face and she'd believed him. She'd thought their fear of her would overwhelm their love of Snow White, but once again she'd been wrong. The diamond shoes glittered on a red velvet cushion. Where was the huntsman now, she wondered? Dead in the forest? Eaten by an owl? Had Snow White's beauty been worth the price he'd paid?

In the corner the cabinet creaked open and, hearing it, Lilith's shoulders slumped. She didn't need this. Not right now. She didn't turn to look at the face she knew would be staring back at her, but drank more wine. She was getting drunk, she knew it. But drunk was good.

'*Snow White is truly the fairest in the land.*'

She ignored it, listening instead to the anger of the storm and the heavy beat of the rain. So Snow White had been woken by true love's kiss. She almost laughed. Good luck to them. If she couldn't see the prince for what he was then she was as foolish as she was beautiful. He was spoiled and vain; that much had been clear from what the raven had shown her. Maybe he was exactly what Snow White deserved.

The girl was finally gone, that was all that mattered.

That was all that should matter.

She drank some more wine.

All she'd wanted was her heart.

12

'If it will make you happy'

It wasn't as hot as the previous day had been and there was a hint of rain in the muggy air, but it was still warm in the village and the prince had left Snow White to bathe while he fetched them some breakfast. He smiled, unable to suppress his happiness. Today, he'd get to go home. It felt as if he'd been away forever and there had been dark moments when he'd thought perhaps his life before had simply been a dream. It was supposed to have been an adventure. Something to prove to his father he was a man once and for all, but the adventure had turned into a nightmare and he'd been lucky to get away alive.

He wondered what had happened to his companion, his guide, but there was no small measure of relief that he would not be returning home with him. Alone, the prince could rewrite the tales he had to tell with no shame at someone else knowing the truth. Not that his companion would ever have said – he was a man of few words – but there was an *honour* about him that would have made the prince feel ashamed of his necessary lies. The story would have to change. He was the prince, after all. And the prince was always the hero.

He wandered through the lively market and bought bread and fruit and some cold meats and then went to the inn kitchen and paid the cook, a warty but warm lady called Maddy, well to finish what he needed and then prepare them a tray. He left her with instructions to send it up to their room shortly. There was no rush. He wanted his princess to enjoy her morning.

Snow White was still in the bath when he returned; he could hear her singing as he passed the washroom. She sounded happy and he was glad about that. He wanted her to be happy. She made him happy. She was *going* to make him happy.

There were roses in the vase on the window ledge and he pulled the petals from the stems and scattered them across the floor and bed. There weren't as many as there would have been for a bride at home – the floor in the palace would have been a sea of them, soft and scented and filling the room with perfume – but it was better than nothing. He took the pink and white dress the dwarves had bought her from its hook in the wardrobe and laid it out on the bed. It was the dress they had met in, after all, and he wanted her to wear it when she arrived in his city.

His heart tightened with love for her and he smiled. He couldn't help it. He waited impatiently.

At last the door opened and she came in wrapped in a thin robe which clung to her hot, damp skin. The dusky patches on her cheeks were shining from the hot water, and her hair was piled up untidily on her head. She paused, noticing the petals under her feet.

'That's very sweet,' she said. 'Thank you.'

He could see the wariness still in her eyes after his coolness of the previous night, but that would pass soon enough.

'I looked for more flowers at the market, but there were none fine enough for you.'

'Oh, I'm sure that's not true.'

'Yes it is.'

She blushed slightly and then saw the dress on the bed. 'You want me to wear this one? I thought you'd want something finer. You know, for meeting your father. It's pretty enough but not, I imagine, the kind of thing the ladies of your castle wear.' She held it up against her. 'And I didn't want to tell Dreamy, but I really hate pink. Maybe we should go back to the dressmaker? See if there's something else?' She chewed her bottom lip again. 'I just want to make a good impression.'

She was nervous of him, he knew. After the awkwardness

of the previous night, he'd expected it.

'But this is what you were wearing when we met. When I first kissed you.' He smiled. 'And that is what I will tell my father, when I tell him all that has happened to you.' He stepped towards her and kissed her on her smooth, pale forehead. 'For me? Please?'

'Okay.' She smiled and shrugged. 'If it will make you happy.'

'Yes.' His heart was racing. 'Yes, it will.'

He turned his back and let her dress with her modesty intact, although she seemed to have no qualms about taking her robe off in front of him, even laughing a little at his good manners after everything they had already done together. She didn't understand, of course. He didn't want to see her like that; earthy and cheap. He wanted his princess back.

'Breakfast, sir?' The voice came from the other side of the door and he pulled it open. The kitchen help stood there, a young boy of maybe fourteen or so. He stared at Snow White, a mixture of lust and awe, but the prince's bride didn't notice how inappropriate it was and simply sent a sweet smile his way.

'Thank you,' she said. 'I'm starving.'

'Just put it on the bed.'

'Yes, sir.' The tray held one glass of juice and one plate with warm bread and jam and some sliced meat and cheese. As the boy closed the door behind him, casting one longing look back at the princess, Snow White frowned.

'Aren't you having any?'

'I ate in the market. I wanted to test it all and make sure it was good enough.'

She laughed again. 'You'll learn that I don't have very fine tastes. I like ordinary things. I always have. They're more real, aren't they?'

She pulled the laces tight on her bodice and then sat on the edge of the bed. 'This looks delicious.' She smiled at him again, her eyes merry and twinkling at last. 'Thank you for everything. For being so kind. And understanding. You didn't have to. I'll be a good wife to you. I promise.'

'It'll be perfect,' he said, and watched as she raised the glass to her lips. There must have been some thing in his expression; a sudden hunger or urgency, because just before the liquid slipped down her throat, her eyes widened in sudden panic and darted sideways. He knew what she was looking at. His money pouch. It sat on the bed, thin and empty. The apple was gone. Crushed up into her glass. She looked back at him, the sparkle in her violet eyes replaced with a terrible sadness, and then the cup tumbled from her hand and spilled its cursed contents onto the floorboards which sucked it up greedily. She fell backwards onto the bed.

He kicked the cup under the bed and then lowered his face close to hers. No breath came from those perfect rosebud lips. Her eyes stared upwards, at nothing and everything.

He stroked her cooling face. The apple was gone. And this time there was no chunk stuck in her throat that could be dislodged. He'd made sure of that by getting the cook to make a juice of it.

'Hello again, my darling,' he whispered, tucking a stray strand of hair carefully behind her ear. 'I've missed you.'

The crowds cheered as their prince returned. Many had presumed him dead and his sudden arrival brought cheer to the kingdom and the streets were filled with music and laughter and banners flying high. The prince had waited at the city walls while a message was sent to the castle in order to give the king's men time to organise his parade. He had no intention of coming back barely noticed. Not after all he'd been through. He was a returning hero. He had the scar to prove it.

He waved at the people as he came through the streets, sitting high and proud on his new steed. Behind him, a few feet back and safely away from prying eyes, a servant followed with the old mule and cart and strict instructions not to look under the blanket. The prince would know if he had. He would see it in his eyes. He'd take care of him as he needed if that was the case. His travels had made him less squeamish. He thought of the dwarves and the reward he'd promised them. He had trusted them too easily. He swallowed the sudden anger that surged through him and leaned down to kiss a milkmaid who'd pushed her way to the front of the crowd. She nearly swooned as he pressed his lips into hers and then pulled away, and her face glowed with excitement. He looked up at the larger houses which lined the streets closer to the castle. On the balconies, finely dressed young women waved handkerchiefs that matched their dresses at him, their eyes flirtatious above the fans that half covered their faces.

It was good to be home. He *would* send something back to the dwarves. They had earned it. But it wouldn't be money or jewellery; it would be an assassin's blade. They had deceived him. They had given him faulty goods. All may have turned out well in the end but that was not down to any action on their part. He did not like to be made a fool of.

Up ahead the crowd roared louder, and he saw that his mother and father had come out onto the castle balcony to greet him. He raised one hand in a salute and his father returned it. The people were almost ecstatic. The prince turned and nodded at the soldier behind him to bring forward the black stallion. The beast wasn't as fully broken as its new owner had been, but that no longer mattered.

The stallion would make an excellent present for the king.

EPILOGUE

The mouse had lost the band of travellers in the forest. He hadn't been able to keep up no matter how fast his little legs carried him. He stood up on his hind legs and sniffed at the air, his whiskers twitching this way and that. Too many scents assailed him, and he couldn't yet tell them apart.

He scurried from bush to bush, keeping close to the ground hoping to avoid the attention of the hungry birds that filled the night skies, hooting and calling to each other as they hunted. Since claws had torn flesh from his back his first night of being cursed, he'd learned to make himself smaller, almost invisible. It was the safest way to be. Now, though, he was close to panic. He knew the edge of the forest must be close, but he was sure he was somehow going in circles. There had been too much change, too much for him to cope with, and when he'd woken under a pile of leaves near the campfire to find the dwarves and Snow White had gone, he'd almost broken. She was his salvation, he was sure of it. Only she might see past his cursed exterior. Only she could perhaps persuade the queen to reverse it.

He was tired and wanted to sleep until daylight but he pushed himself onwards. To pause would be to admit defeat and he couldn't do that. Something white glimmered suddenly on the path ahead. He trembled and moved closer, his small nose quivering. Bread. It was bread. He nibbled a corner and it was thick and fresh. His tiny dark eyes shone as he looked further ahead. He could see another piece perhaps ten feet ahead. He ran towards it, his feet silent on the forest floor. Up ahead, another. His heart lifted. A breadcrumb trail. He ran back into the safety of the falling leaves but followed the path someone had left for him which finally took him to the forest's edge. A new adventure was just beginning.

Finally back at home, the old lady soaked her feet, a mass of corns and bunions, in a bucket of warm water as she sat by the fire. It had been a long few days, but she smiled contentedly. It had been good to get out. She'd enjoyed messing in the business of the world a little. It made her feel alive again. It had been too many long years since she'd ventured beyond the forest, and it had been invigorating. And always good to see little Lilith. Lilith with the lisp as she'd been so many years ago.

She let her old bones settle and creak back into the chair and watched the flames dance. The house had been cold when she'd got back but it would soon warm up. The large oven was back on and soon her cottage would be toasty warm again. Yes, it had been good to get out, but it was always lovely to be home.

She thought of the breadcrumbs she'd left for the mouse. He'd find them. She was sure of that. She'd also dropped breadcrumbs all the way home too. She wasn't even sure why, she just had nothing else to do with the bread she supposed. Bread had never really agreed with her, she just liked the smell of it baking. Gave her wind whenever she ate it.

She dozed a little and then, just as the fire began to die down, she roused herself and got up to close the curtains.

And there they were.

Two children.

'Look! Look! This is where the bread leads!'

'Is that fence made of chocolate?'

Giggles. Whispers.

She bent her back over, made herself look frail and

prepared herself for visitors. She was happy. She peered out between the gap in the curtains. A boy and a girl. Not too young but not too old. And the little boy was decidedly chubby. She smiled and her mouth watered. She'd earned a good dinner.

THE END

ABOUT THE AUTHOR

Sarah Pinborough is a critically acclaimed horror, thriller and YA author. She has written for *New Tricks* on the BBC and has an original horror film in development. Sarah won the British Fantasy Award for Best Novella with *Beauty* in 2013, Best Short Story in 2009, and has three times been short-listed for Best Novel. She has also been short-listed for a World Fantasy Award.

www.sarahpinborough.com

Also available from

SARAH PINBOROUGH & TITAN BOOKS

Charm

A Wicked *Cinderella* Tale

Beauty

A Wicked *Sleeping Beauty* Tale

For more fantastic fiction, author events, exclusive
excerpts, competitions, limited editions and more

VISIT OUR WEBSITE
titanbooks.com

LIKE US ON FACEBOOK
facebook.com/titanbooks

FOLLOW US ON TWITTER
@TitanBooks

EMAIL US
readerfeedback@titanemail.com